the waiting booth

Whispering Woods #1

Brinda Berry

Copyright Warning

Published By Sweet Biscuit Publishing LLC
Cover Design by Najla Qamber Designs

The Waiting Booth
All Rights Are Reserved. Copyright 2011 by Brinda Berry

First electronic publication: July 2011 by Etopia Press

Second electronic publication: October 2014 by Sweet Biscuit Publishing LLC

First print publication: October 2014

Digital ISBN: 978-0-9916320-6-0

Print ISBN: 978-0692316979

About the Author

Brinda Berry lives in the South with her family and two spunky cairn terriers. She's terribly fond of chocolate, coffee, and books that take her away from reality. She doesn't mind being called a geek or "crazy dog lady." When she's not working the day job or writing a novel, she's guilty of surfing the internet for no good reason.

Social media at:

http://www.brindaberry.com
https://www.facebook.com/BrindaBerryAuthor
https://twitter.com/#!/Brinda_Berry

For release news, subscribe at

http://www.brindaberry.com/mailing-list.html

Dedication

For my sister Audrey, who read it first and never let me doubt.

Chapter One

Mystery

My new life began on a Saturday. It was a life that chose me, which shouldn't have been surprising. A real shocker would be gliding through my senior year without one more thing to label my life dysfunctional. Most seventeen-year-olds would have called the events a headon collision. For me, I was merely sideswiped in the journey to find my missing brother.

Saturday mornings were always my favorite. Dad cooked pancakes for the two of us and that day the vanilla-laden smell wafted up the stairs and tugged at my stomach. I bounded downstairs in my shorts and "Geek Chic" T-shirt, sliding around the slick corner reminiscent of the way Tom Cruise did in Dad's favorite old movie, *Risky Business*. And he looked up, spatula in hand, with that same welcoming smile full of comfort and familiarity.

I inhaled deeply. "Yum." I sat down and picked up

my

fork in anticipation. A golden-brown stack waited on the serving platter.

My dad pulled on my ponytail before taking a seat across from me. He stared at the empty chair to my right. I concentrated on my plate.

We both helped ourselves to generous mounds of pancakes, and then I drizzled enough maple syrup to drive me into a sugar coma. The only sound filling the kitchen was the smacking and fork scraping that indicate true culinary delight.

As usual, my eyes were bigger than my stomach. I shook my head woefully at the butter- and syrup-laced masterpiece I was abandoning. I rose and cleared my plate from the table.

"Hold up. You in a hurry?" Dad asked.

"Gotta go get my memory cards out of the cameras outside and see if I got anything recorded," I answered in between licking my sticky lips.

I slipped on my tennis shoes and went for the door. "Leaving Biscuit here?" Dad looked down. My cairn terrier sat expectantly at Dad's feet. Biscuit wagged his stubby tail when he heard his name. I grinned at his pitiful face, black button eyes hopeful for a few stray crumbs. "Yeah, I'll be right back. He can stay with you." Biscuit looked from Dad to me before settling his chin on his paws.

I ran out the door and hopped into the old golf cart that sat in the garage. Even though I had gotten my license last year, I still preferred the golf cart for these errands. The aging motor started immediately and then I was off. I puttered down the long gravel driveway toward the highway.

The early morning air was crisp, and the sun hadn't risen high enough to warm the areas beneath the canopy of oak trees. Enjoying my time alone in the woods, I breathed in the fragrant air. The smells of pine and cedar and the sounds of stirring intensified all the green colors of the leaves. But that was how I always saw things. The doctors had diagnosed my older brother as also having synesthesia. They quoted statistics of the number of people who experienced the same condition. And Pete never gave me away.

I wasn't happy about being like Pete. I didn't care if Mozart, Stevie Wonder, Billy Joel, and a lot of other talented people belonged to the synesthesia club. The famous ones had obviously figured out useful talents for the strange way we viewed the world. I didn't feel gifted. Cursed was more like it. My sensory perception overlapped and hit me like a Mack truck every day.

The words on my homework invited my eyes to revel in their watercolor loveliness. The chalkboard became a living, breathing Matisse canvas. Music class exhausted me in the efforts to appear as bored and sleepy as my classmates. Each note enveloped my senses in vibrant greens, reds, and blues. I wanted sounds to be sounds and not a rush of colors invading my brain like a psychedelic avalanche.

The birds chirped and frissons tingled down my spine. Squirrels stirred the brittle leaves. I concentrated on the task ahead and ignored the symphony. It didn't take long to drive around and retrieve the memory cards from the outdoor cameras and replace each with a blank card.

I went back inside the house and returned to the sanctuary of my room. The morning light streamed through the window. I sank onto my bed, closing my eyes and breathing deeply of silence and stillness. I huddled beneath a soft cotton pillow over my head. Dark, cool, nothing.

Thirty minutes later, I got out of bed and stuck the first memory card in the slot of my computer. To my surprise, there were a total of forty-five pictures. "Yes!" I pumped my fist. I opened the first file and my photo software displayed a clear picture of two cute raccoons eating from the plot across from the mounted camera. Cool. I'd been prepared to be a little disappointed, but I had already scored.

Scrolling through the rest of the pictures, I made notes in my logbook of the current moon phase. I noted the time lapse and approximate feeding time recorded as well as listing raccoon, deer, and birds as the animal subjects. My photos displayed a virtual Discovery Channel scene down there.

I examined the second memory card marked "b" with a black Sharpie pen to indicate the location. This particular camera had recorded the activity at the waiting booth, my favorite childhood haven, still sitting at the end of the driveway. I inserted it into the card slot and drummed my fingers on the desk. The files opened with fewer pictures recorded by the motion-activated camera. I scrolled through the first three pictures and really couldn't see anything. Dang.

I wondered what had activated the sensor to begin taking pictures. I hit the arrow key to continue scrolling through the files. Third picture.

Nothing.
Fourth picture.
Nada.
I sighed, already bored and wondering who might be online to chat. I quickly tapped the arrow key several times in quick succession.

"Whoa," I said and sat forward, nearly slipping off the edge of my seat.

I squinted to make sure I wasn't seeing things. A guy stood at the right edge of the photo. The image resolution was clear; nevertheless, I zoomed in to take a closer look and could see that there were actually two people. I clicked the forward button to display the next photo.

Nothing.

The twelfth photo was the last on the memory card. I hit the back button. Why in the world was someone near the waiting booth in the middle of the night? I looked again at the photo to see if I recognized the person. I know everyone in Whispering Woods High School. With a school population of three hundred, that was pretty easy. This guy was definitely not someone I knew. He looked like he could be my age or older. Maybe he was a college student. There were literally thousands of students attending Whispering Woods U.

I called Austin. I was glad to have an excuse to call. We hadn't been speaking since he had blown a fuse because I couldn't go to GameCon. I didn't like holding grudges.

"Hi."

"Hey, I thought you might be mad at me. I shouldn't have said that about your dad."

"Forget it. I know you didn't mean it," I answered, although I was sure that he did. I rolled my eyes, glad that he couldn't see me through the phone.

After a silence during which I imagined him thinking of a way to invite himself over, I said, "Listen, I have some pics from the camera down at the booth, and there's a guy in one. Actually, I think there're two guys. I think they're guys..."

Silence hung like a thick fog while Austin absorbed what I had said. Because my dad and I lived on approximately one hundred acres of woods, we rarely happened upon people wandering around on our land. The waiting booth sat at the end of the long drive near the public road, but that still didn't explain the presence of a person in the middle of the night.

"You're messing with me, right? Chainsaw murderers hanging out at the waiting booth?" Austin then started humming the music from *the Friday the 13th* movies. "I'm coming over. Don't go down there without me."

I smiled because he couldn't be mad if he was ordering me around. "Sure, Austin. I've been down to the camera already to get the memory card. I mean, you know that they're long gone."

"I'm on my way," Austin said in an excited voice.

The call clicked off.

I looked back at my computer screen. "My dad is fine," I said to the machine when I remembered Austin's last comments to me when we had talked last night. I had known that he would be aggravated, but he had crossed the line in dissing my dad. "Maybe you're the one who should get a girlfriend," I said as if Austin could hear me.

The problem was that I think he wanted me to be that person. Ever since Austin had awkwardly tried to kiss me about a week ago, I had been weirded out. I'd turned my head so his lips had met my cheek, but I sensed that he'd planned the kiss differently. I shook my head to shake the image.

The mid-morning light in my room was bright, and I closed the blinds to see images on the screen clearer. The profile of the guy in the picture would be difficult for Austin to identify. The camera took infrared photos, everything in black and white.

Wearing jeans and a jacket, the first person looked like half of the people my age in Whispering Woods. Actually, the weather was too warm for a jacket at this time of year, so that told me that he wasn't from around here or he was dressing that way to look cute for somebody. Either way, he didn't have good sense. Arkansas was hot in September and wearing those clothes would make you melt like a toddler's ice cream cone.

The picture was a side profile shot. I started doodling notes on my pad: 1. medium length dark hair, 2. taller than the second person, 3. carrying something. He probably didn't even realize that his picture had been taken. The second person was partially blocked, so there wasn't even enough to scribble a note about him or her.

The thought of someone lurking at the end of my road made a shiver of cold dance along my spine. Jeepers creepers. Had I looked in the garage to see if thieves had taken something? No, of course I hadn't. Maybe they'd been driving around and for some reason had gotten out of their car.

Fifteen minutes later, the doorbell rang. I yelled, "Coming," as I ran down the stairs. I could see my dad opening the door.

"Hi, Mr. Taylor. Mia here?" Austin entered without waiting to be invited in.

My dad stepped aside and looked up at me expectantly as I was taking the last few steps. I hoped that Austin wouldn't breathe a word about what was on the pictures. I sure didn't want my dad to be paranoid about leaving me alone during the week while he worked out of town.

"Dad, Austin's helping me with my science project. Come on up."

My dad had always liked Austin. If he ever found out that Austin had hit on me, that would change in a heartbeat. For crying out loud, I even thought about Austin like he was a brother. That he'd tried to kiss me sent the ick factor into the stratosphere.

We bounded up the stairs as quickly as possible without alerting my dad to some urgency in the air. I closed the door behind Austin and proceeded to move my computer mouse to bring the screen back in view.

Austin looked at the picture as he sat at my desk chair. "And this was the one at the end of your driveway?"

"Yeah," I answered, hoping he would tell me he knew the guy, and he wasn't some ax murderer roaming my woods.

"Pretty good pic," Austin muttered. He clicked to zoom in on the face. "Still...it's hard to make him out."

"Do you recognize him or not?"

"Nope. Can't say I know him. It's not like I know everybody. It's a big school. And he might not even be a college student. I can barely tell anything about the second person." Austin clicked the forward and back buttons in the photo software program. "Why are they only in one frame?"

"I guess they're really fast. I have the timer set to take a picture every six seconds after motion activation."

He nodded. "Let's go down and take a gander. Maybe they dropped something. Or maybe we can figure out why they were down there."

Austin led the way out of my room while I covertly studied him. If I tried to forget that he was like a brother to me, I could see that he was good-looking. He was a little on the lanky side, and that made him look younger to most people. His dark hair always hung into his eyes, which made him seem a little derelict. His new sword tattoo covered about two inches of his right forearm. I had tried to talk him out of it, but he had grinned and said that I'd want one exactly like it.

He looked back at me as I stood there and smiled a *I just caught you checking me out* grin. I wasn't really looking at him like that, but I felt myself blush and quickly found something else to focus on as I followed him out the door.

We left the house and took Austin's car to the waiting booth. He drove an old black Jeep that was still minus the shell since the weather was warm enough. We jumped out to examine the area. On the same side of the drive as the wooden structure, saplings tangled with briars and brush as far as the eye could see. In the years before I was able to drive myself to school, my dad had kept the area fairly clean and bare with the aid of a tractor. Now, this area had become overgrown and weedy.

In the middle of the stalks of high grass, a circle of flattened brush marked where the people in the photo had been standing. "Holy cow, you'd really have to be dragging something heavy to make this dent in the ground." I gasped, suspecting that the marks were new and the people in the photo had created them.

Austin walked around the flattened circle. "This is too weird. See how the grass swirls in a pattern? Maybe that dude had set something down here."

"He wasn't dragging anything in the picture. Maybe I need to look at it again." I estimated the diameter of the circle to be about five feet across. I caught my breath as I felt a reverberating tickle pluck my spine like a tightly wound cello string. Avoiding the circle, I walked into the brush past it to see if I could find more evidence of the intruders. Nothing.

The weather had been fairly dry with no rain this month, but I bent to look for footprints. I started feeling silly, because even if I found footprints, I wouldn't be able to tell anything from them. I shivered, trying to rid myself of the willies.

"They walked this way." Austin pointed at a place the brush was parted in a small area.

Wow. I was impressed. I rose to follow him, relieved to leave behind the vibrating sound that filled my ears and set my nerves on edge. Austin seemed oblivious to my discomfort.

"Cool. I didn't know you were such a Boy Scout." I said with genuine admiration.

"Babe, I have skills you don't even know about," he said. I could see his head swelling.

"Oh, really, Boy Scout... Lead on," I said with a smile. "And Austin, don't call me babe."

Austin stumbled over some low-lying brambles that had caught his shoe. I followed as he made his way through the gap that seemed to be obvious now that he had discovered it. I carefully walked past a briar bush that threatened to snag at my legs, bare below shorts. Austin had on jeans and tennis shoes, so he stomped through trying to enlarge the path for me.

The thicket suddenly opened to a small clearing.

Looking down, Austin nodded and pointed at the ground. "Tire tracks." The thin tire marks in the soft ground ran parallel and led eastward.

"Motorcycles?" I asked as I looked at Austin for confirmation. "I knew they didn't walk in. But why would they hide them?" I said to myself as much as to Austin.

Austin was staring at me. "You're not telling your dad, are you." A statement, not a question. We both knew that my dad would freak out if he thought someone had even been on our land without his permission. My dad worked as a computer security analyst and had recently taken on a new government contract. The more successful he became, the more he had to leave our house.

"No way."

After Pete had disappeared, Dad had become

protective though Pete had been labeled a runaway. We knew that wasn't true. My dad had spent over two years searching online and through nearby cities for a clue to Pete's whereabouts.

"I was kind of freaked out earlier, but it's not a big deal," I continued. "I have the alarm system on the house, and it's probably nothing."

"I don't like it," Austin set both his hands on my shoulders and looked me in the eyes. "I want you to call me if anything spooks you."

I disengaged myself from his hold. "You know I will." I steadied my emotions and took a deep breath. I didn't like being told what to do, even by my friends. "They probably stole the bikes and hid them here until they could come back for them. Or something like that."

I didn't even believe that story, but I really had no reasonable explanation that would put Austin's mind at rest. "Come on, I need to look at the rest of the memory cards and work on my project," I said. "You can hang for a little while if you want to. My dad won't care."

We drove back to the house in silence. I tried to come up with plausible explanations for the guys in my woods and the motorcycle tracks. The more I thought about it, the better my fabricated explanation sounded.

Austin spent the morning on my desk computer while I browsed through the rest of the photos on my laptop. Periodically, he would glance over to see what photos had been taken as if half expecting the two mysterious strangers to show up in some more footage. I logged my results with satisfaction, copied the photos onto my hard drive, and formatted the cards to replace the next ones I switched out to view.

Finished with my tasks for my science project, I lay across my bed and tucked a pillow under my chin to watch Austin play *Quest of Zion*. Ignoring me, his attention to the screen was intense as he maneuvered his avatar across the wooded terrain of the playing environment.

A beep alerted me that a text had arrived on my cell. "What u doin?" said Em.

"Hangin out with Austin. Wanna come over?" I replied with the speed that comes with hours of texting.

"B there in half hour."

Austin leaned back in my computer chair, his socked feet resting on the edge of my bed, and studied my face. "Listen, about GameCon. I was outta line saying that about your dad. I really wanted you to go."

"Yeah, I know. And I think I was in a funk yesterday. I've started thinking about Pete a lot. It's been a while since I let that get me down."

He hesitated as if choosing his words carefully, "I miss your brother, too, but you can't be sad every time you think about him. I have to believe that he's fine. You should think like that too or it's gonna eat you up, you know?"

"I wasn't sad. I just remembered how much I miss him. The booth does that to me."

"That bench down there?"

"I can remember sitting down there with Pete waiting on the bus." I smiled. "Pete would get into a fight with me over something stupid and then he would make up with me by giving me the cookies from his lunch."

My throat tightened, but I would not cry. I wouldn't. I sat up and hugged the pillow to my chest.

"I'm glad you can talk about it. I remember when you wouldn't." He sat on the bed beside me. Because my throat was tight, I couldn't say a word in fear that the floodgate of tears would open. He tugged the pillow from my arms and settled a comforting arm around me, which was the worst thing he could do. I extended my hand to push his chest away and stop him from comforting me.

"Knock, knock." My dad opened the door.

I pushed away from Austin quickly. My cheeks flushed, and Austin scurried back to the desk chair. He was grinning uncomfortably as though he realized how bad we looked. I wanted to literally shove him back into that chair.

This was the last thing I needed. My dad had never been leery of Austin hanging out at our house all the time.

Dad cleared his throat, "How's the science project going?" He sounded calm.

I tried to act casual. Austin grinned like an idiot, and I contemplated how to deflect the situation. Wow, this looked bad.

"Dad, could you not come busting in my room unannounced?" I asked.

The grin disappeared from Austin's face. Uh-oh.

Dad shook his head, and his mouth formed a straight parental line. "Mia, when you turn thirty, you can lock that door. For now, I'll ask that you act like you expect me to enter at any time."

"Sure, Dad. Austin was just giving me a hug to cheer me up. We were talking about Pete." And that last sentence changed my dad's face. I wasn't manipulating my dad. I knew that the truth was best.

"OK, kids," he answered with relief. Apparently I wasn't the only one who didn't want to think of Austin as boyfriend material. "Listen, I wanted to tell you that I'm making homemade pizza for lunch. Austin, you're going to stay, right?"

The doorbell rang, and my dad nodded reassuringly at Austin as if to say, *Everything is cool with us.*

"That's probably Em. I forgot all about her," I said as I exited the room and ran down the stairs.

Em stood in the doorway holding her laptop and a brown paper bag. It had to be the usual bag of candy from the Gas-Up Quik Stop. She'd braided her long hair into pigtails, copying her fave teen models. I thought she looked like a mischievous kid. As I neared, she opened the screen door, peeking her head into the room.

I waved at her to hurry.

"Hey you. My favorite friend who always knows just what to bring when she comes over." I took the bag out of her hands.

Dad, who'd followed me down the stairs, tugged Em's pigtail. I groaned in embarrassment for Em since he had basically told her that her hairstyle was probably closer to a five-year-old's.

"Hi, Mr. Taylor," Em murmured.

"I am so glad you're here, Emily. You can chaperone up there so I won't have to walk in on a make out session again," my dad said.

Em's eyes widened and her mouth dropped. So gullible.

"Oh, Em," I was a little irritated. "He's kidding."

"Pizza in an hour." My dad walked toward the kitchen. He tended to cook a lot on the weekends. I didn't know if he did it because he liked cooking or he was making up for the lack of home-cooked meals throughout the week.

Austin stood in my bedroom doorway. "Em, you gotta see Mia's pictures from her camera. We caught some dudes hangin' out in the woods."

"Really? How scary," Em shrilled, the energy of her voice pulsing in like a pink frisson around her.

I pushed the sensation down. "Shhh..." I closed the door swiftly. "I'm trying to make sure my dad doesn't know and freak out. He'll rearrange his work schedule, and he's been traveling this month."

Austin was searching the memory card files in an attempt to view the picture.

Em leaned over to look at the picture as he found the correct one and enlarged it. "Wow. I mean it's so clear. Scoot over Austin, I wanna mess with it." Em was totally comfortable with me and Austin but was a little bit of an introvert with other people our age. And of the three of us, Emily was actually more of a techie, so Austin immediately did what she asked.

Em opened some photo software. "I'm going to add some fill light and sharpen. I won't change your original, but we may be able to see their faces better."

She zoomed in to focus on the people in the photo, then clicked the mouse swiftly, executing photo editing that would put the professionals to shame.

She sat back in satisfaction and grinned. "He's cute, Mia. No wonder you've been hiding him here."

"Very funny," I replied.

Austin rolled his eyes with a sour look. "Zoom in on the second person... Good job, Em, I can see that this one's for sure a dude. I thought this was a shadow, but I think he needs to shave." He pointed at the darkened profile.

"He doesn't look too bad either, Mia." Em continued her teasing, oblivious to Austin's reaction.

"We found motorcycle tracks and a clearing where they had hidden them," I said.

Em's dimples appeared with an impish grin. "Cool, love a guy on a motorcycle."

"Cool? If my dad catches them on our land, he's likely to go ballistic."

"If I catch 'em, there's gonna be hell to pay," Austin grumbled.

Em and I exchanged a knowing look. Guys have to feel that they are big and bad. I guess it's harmless to let men have their delusions. I would have bet Emily a month's allowance that Austin had never even been in a fight.

"Yeah," I said, trying to keep a serious face. "We'll count them lucky. I think that the motorcycles were stolen, and they're long gone."

***

My dad called us down for lunch, and we stuffed ourselves with his "everything but the kitchen sink" pizza. I sat on the bar stool across from my friends and laughed at Austin's stories about his summer senior trip with the guys. While some people collected hats or mugs, Austin collected stories. He seemed to have a bottomless well of tall tales that always made me smile. I didn't care if the stories were true or not. They were always funny.

We spent the rest of the afternoon in my room listening to music and talking. Em informed us that her parents had definitely said "no" to a trip alone with Austin. I wasn't surprised to hear it.

Austin's appearance tended to scare some parents, and although my dad knew that he was harmless, others weren't sure. Austin had developed a look with his haircut, or lack of, and clothes that said, "Don't mess with me." I really thought he was all bark and no bite. The latest addition of the tattoo was the final touch to his rebel appearance. Lots of kids were getting tattoos these days as soon as they were of age. People in Whispering Woods were old-fashioned. But even my grandfather has a massive dragon tattoo he got during his years in the service.

Although Austin really wanted us to go to GameCon, he didn't seem too upset at me and for that, I was glad.

After Em and Austin left, I spent the rest of my Saturday night watching movies with my dad. The peaceful hum of the ceiling fan whirred and filled my mind with white wispy feathers of comfort. He fell asleep in his recliner, and I spread a sofa blanket over him before turning off the lamps and tiptoeing away. I closed and locked the doors, turned on the alarm system, and went upstairs with Biscuit.

Chapter Two

Regulus

Whispering Woods University's bookstore was crowded with students who were halfheartedly studying their schedules, looking for books, and evaluating the dating possibilities of the incoming class. The scent of hormonal overdrive hung thickly in the air. Regulus frowned as he listened to an overzealous type talk loudly about a party he planned to crash.

"Oh, sorry," a brunette said breathily as she bumped his arm.

Regulus looked at her flushed face and the wide, empty aisle. He smiled and said, "No problem." He relocated to the opposite side and pretended to become engrossed by the pamphlet in his hand.

The girl stood inches away and tried to see what he was reading.

Regulus glanced up, smiled again, and turned to

look for Arizona, who was talking with a girl while he examined a book. Regulus frowned as he approached them, waiting for a break in the conversation.

"So, you think that this teacher never really uses the book and only tests from the notes?" Arizona said.

"Sure. The old hag likes to see us spend all our money so we're broke for the rest of the semester. I swear, I don't remember one question ever coming from that book. I stopped studying from it after the second test." The girl jutted her hip out and stuck her hand on it for emphasis.

"How could I not trust a pretty girl like you? I think I'll wait to buy it." Arizona smiled brilliantly. He even winked at her, which seemed a little over the top, but she was so enthralled it seemed to pass right by her.

"Arizona, we should be going now," Regulus said. He'd been taught that patience was the key to all successful endeavors, but he failed to see the benefit of Arizona's conversation with this female. Regulus looked at her bleached blonde hair, her makeup-enhanced face, and short skirt. He knew she met the definition of "hot," but he felt unaffected by her. He continued, "Your girlfriend said you have to be back in thirty minutes or she's coming to look for you."

Arizona glared at Regulus. He turned to the pretty girl who had stopped twirling her long hair with her finger and nodded. As they walked away, Arizona said, "There's no harm in research, Regulus. Looking for mates is an acceptable sport here. It can be fun."

"No time for fun. Did you get the information? I could hear your conversation with the girl and that wasn't it."

"They're not going to confide in strangers. I can't help it if I'm extremely skilled at it."

Regulus looked at him sternly. "You know it's forbidden, Arizona. Don't bring us in a situation where
I have to cover for you."

"I'm talking with a girl. Not a relationship...there's a difference. I know the consequences better than anyone." Arizona spat the words out and nervously rubbed his right wrist.

"The temptation is too great in there for you," Regulus said laughing, trying to lighten the situation.

"You're right. They've thrown me into the gene pool. But we'd both better get used to it here. These people don't think about much else."

Regulus answered without hesitation, "I won't have any difficulties with it."

Chapter Three

Caught Again

I preferred to hang out with guys until they decide that I'm a girl. Then they get all weird on me. Today, Austin was definitely getting on my nerves. Apparently, standing and watching me work was entertaining.

"You should install that lower. You know that squirrels are the only thing you'll get here," Austin muttered. His irritated tone washed over me in browns as the buzzing I always heard near the booth grew in intensity. I ignored him.

I looked away from Austin to examine the small shelter in front. I needed to concentrate on getting finished with my task, which was difficult with his stare burning a hole through me. Looking at the place where I had attached the wildlife camera, I shook my head. I had originally thought that the roof of the waiting booth would be a great place. I pushed my fingertips against a piece of wood on the structure to test it and frowned at the dilapidated state. The red paint that had once covered the wood was now reduced to small slivers of pink that were peeling and rubbing off with the pressure of my fingers. I guess I hadn't noticed its deterioration over the years. I would be lucky if the camera didn't fall off.

"Why doesn't your dad tear this old thing down?" Austin persistently attempted conversation.

"He would never do that," I said, trying to keep the anger out of my voice. "You know that my dad built it for me and Pete to wait for the bus here." That really wouldn't be an explanation to most people, but Austin should understand the significance.

"No, I wouldn't tear it down either."

I looked down at my cairn terrier and cooed to my faithful friend, "Dad wouldn't get rid of the waiting booth, would he now? It's practically a historical landmark. Where else would you hide when I'm trying to find you?"

Biscuit wagged his tail.

Austin shook his long bangs out of his eyes and bent down at eye level with the dog. "Come here, boy."

Biscuit turned away and hopped up on the seat of the old golf cart. Austin gave me a dirty look as if I had cued Biscuit, and I shrugged.

"So your hypothesis is, people tend to spook around in the woods at night, and if you get them on film..."

"I'm testing whether moon phases influence the feeding patterns of wildlife. I planted some small plots of peas and clover over the summer. My outdoor cameras are motion activated so if a deer or anything feeds at any time, I'll get it recorded. I'll collect my SD cards everyday and check them for activity."

"So, what are we gonna do about the dude in the picture?" Austin asked. "You can't turn it into the police or your dad will know." He seemed to be trying to be helpful. Or at least the words indicated that to me.

"Austin, the guy in the picture was a fluke. I'm sure we'll never see him and the other person again. I'm not going to worry about it. Did you know that Dr. Bleeker said this project could win at the science fair if I do it right?"

Austin came over to me, his flip-flops raising dust with each step he took. Biscuit barked sharply and stood up on the old cart seat. I shushed him, but he stood with his ears perked at attention. Eying the dog, Austin slowly sat on the waiting booth bench to my left. The wooden bench was short, and we took up the entire space.

He swept his bangs to one side and peered at me through the strands of dark hair that lay over one eye. "Did you ask your dad to change his mind about GameCon?"

I hesitated to answer, because I knew Austin was going to be unhappy about my lack of initiative. "Not yet."

Austin nodded. "I think you should try again since he's had time to think about it. You never get in any trouble, and he knows you're safe with me and Em. He overreacts sometimes because of Pete disappearing, but you're not Pete." He slouched over and rested his elbows on his jean-clad knees. Frowning, he said, "What's up with Biscuit? He seems like he's about to jump me. He's acting like a psycho dog."

He leaned back and crossed one ankle over his knee as he draped his arm over the back of the bench. My dog growled.

"Biscuit!" I guessed something was bothering him today, too. Or maybe he could sense my agitation and that Austin was getting pushy. Austin and I would always be friends, but lately I had the definite and undesired feeling that he was seeing us as more than friends. "I think maybe he's tired since he has been running around. You know during the week he literally sleeps all day. I hooked up one camera in the house to make sure that I knew how to use it. Biscuit slept about eight hours while I was at school. Oh, and he spent fifteen minutes at the window barking."

I stood and stretched. Biscuit started to growl again. He jumped off the cart seat and bounded to a spot directly across from us. His carrot tail stuck straight up as he furiously ran circles in an area the size of an ice chest. I looked to see what he had discovered, but there was nothing there. Austin slung his arm out to stop me from moving.

"Maybe he's found a snake. I'll do it."

I rolled my eyes and went to pick up my dog. If there was a snake, I would be rescuing my dog myself and not waiting for some guy to come to my aid. I marched forward before Austin could to get Biscuit. The air suddenly came alive with buzzing and movement. My nostrils were filled with the fresh smell of a lake in the early morning hours. I managed to grab Biscuit, who was running around me. I could vaguely hear Austin's voice in the background. He led me back to the bench holding the squirming dog in one arm while using the other to help me.

"You OK?" He looked really worried.

"I'm fine," I answered, exasperated with his smothering. "Listen, thanks for everything, but I need to head to the house. You're the one who's overreacting."

Austin wouldn't look me in the eye. I could tell I had hurt his feelings. Since when had he gotten so sensitive? Or maybe he was acting fine today, and I was the moody one. I felt remorseful that I had been sharp with Austin. He and Emily had been there for me when Pete had disappeared.

A year ago, the police had labeled my older brother Pete as a runaway. My dad and I didn't believe that for one minute, but the event helped me see my true friends... things had gotten crazy. I had relied upon them for my sanity in the past year and would never forget the safety of their friendship. I was sure that without them, life would have been really bad.

"I'll be online later tonight. How about I log on to play *Quest of Zion* around seven and look for you?"

He smiled then. "Yeah, I'll probably be on," he answered. "I'll text Em and tell her what time."

I slid into the golf cart, still carrying Biscuit. I turned the key in the starter when Austin added, "Don't forget to ask your dad again about going to Dallas for GameCon weekend. I know you can turn on that charm and get him to change his mind."

I nodded and started the cart.

Austin swung one leg over the seat of his fourwheeler. "Later... Peace out." He grinned and noisily started the ATV before giving it more gas than necessary and speeding off. He'd take only a few minutes to get home at the speed he was going. He loved to go fast, although he knew that I got nervous when he drove too fast.

I drove up the gravel drive with Biscuit perched in my lap, staying under ten miles per hour. I couldn't go fast in the cart on the gravel road, but it sure beat walking. The gravel drive was a nice path to the house, but the ride was long and uphill. I immediately felt more relaxed as I drove away from the waiting booth. I had let the last half hour rattle me.

The sunlight made patterns through the trees overhead, dappling the road in a mosaic of light and dark. Sweetgum, red maple, and dogwood trees lined the drive as if my dad had planted each one in a strategic outlay of color and breadth. Of course, he hadn't planted any of the trees as Mother Nature was the gardener in our woods. The leaves were still various shades of green since the summer warmth still lingered in the September air. Soon, the weather would perform its magic, and the chrysalis effect of reds and oranges would emerge. I was comforted to see colors I knew were real and not a figment of my imagination.

Home, I turned off the golf cart's engine and coasted into the garage beside my dad's car. The small area was crowded with boxes marked Xerox Paper stacked in a perilously haphazard fashion. The boxes held the belongings that my mother had left behind. Evidently, she didn't want to be reminded of the average life she had in Whispering Woods—you know, the three bedroom home nicely equipped with husband and two children. Or in our case, make that two children and a dog.

For years I had thought of those boxes as a symbol of her disregard of us and a need for a clean, neat getaway. I had wanted to throw everything out, but I finally understood why mom's things remained after Pete had disappeared. My aunt Candy had suggested that we clean out Pete's room. Donate things to Goodwill. I refused to see anything changed in his room. That's when I understood.

After dinner, I walked up the stairs of the only home I had ever known. I didn't plan on leaving Whispering Woods to attend college. We had a great university right here.

I shook my head in bewilderment as I took each step, thinking about my dad's continuous lectures. He wanted me to attend colleges like Brown and Columbia. I had toured these schools and applied, but I secretly crossed my fingers that they'd lose my application. I belonged right here.

I looked down at the wood planks of the stairs, which had dulled under foot traffic. At the top of the staircase, I quickened my step and entered my sanctuary. My room was at odds with the woodsy decor in the rest of the house. My dad didn't care what I hung on the walls or how messy my room might be. I had hand-me-down posters of video game heroes that Pete had given me on every wall.

I turned on selected lamps, since I preferred dim lighting while I worked on my computer for hours every night. The sounds of cicadas wafted in through my open window. The room was shadowy, and the night sounds were pleasantly soothing. I was given a new laptop last Christmas, so I wasn't tied to working at my desk. Nevertheless, my desk still housed my gaming computer that Austin had helped me to build.

I sat in front of my desktop PC. The *Quest of Zion* site requested my login info and the menu appeared. I clicked on the "Pub" icon, which was the message board for players. No messages, so I proceeded to enter the game. A side panel displayed my guild of friends who were online and offline at the moment. Austin and Em were both already visible as online.

A chat message popped into the bottom of the panel from Super Girl, alias Em, "Did you check the pictures from your outdoor camera today?"

"No," I typed. "Why?"

"Wanted to know if you got some gr8 pics with that guy again," Em said.

"Highly unlikely."

I grabbed the memory card from the waiting booth and inserted it. I started moving my avatar in Quest forward to select weapons as the photo software started in another window on the screen. My virtual warrior picked a sickle, to challenge my skills. What damage could I do with that? I wondered. I thought about Pete and wished he were here to tell me about it.

I glanced at the photo software window and gasped. A clear view of my mystery subject was in the frame. I enlarged the photo full screen, ignoring the battle that had started on Quest. It wasn't necessary to do any manipulation as Em had performed yesterday. The image was clear. The two guys were close to the camera and facing it.

I recognized the one with dark hair from yesterday's pictures. I thought about how black and white pictures tended to blur out the imperfections as I looked at his face. Wow. He didn't look like an ax murderer. He was smiling, and I was mesmerized by his beautiful smile and white teeth. And dimples. I scolded myself for drooling over the picture. The other guy had blond hair and was as attractive. His hair was longer and made me think of surfer guys, although we didn't have any in Whispering Woods.

Oddly enough, I wasn't scared that the guys were in my woods a second night. What were they doing out there?

***

Dad had packed his travel bag and left our house for his red-eye flight. He usually flew out late Sunday night when he had to be on-site for a project Monday morning so he could spend more time with me, though he declared that he liked to sleep during travel and found the timing better for that.

Ten o'clock... I had a busy school week mapped on my scheduler. After checking that out, I performed the nightly routine of securing the house and arming the alarm. I was tempted to stay up for some online gaming, but decided to resist and hit the hay. I had snuggled underneath my favorite cotton quilt when Biscuit decided to be mischievous. Normally, he jumped into bed with me and stayed quiet all night.

Now, he scratched at the downstairs door while I wished for a doggie door. I had suggested it once, and then dad had reminded me of the "presents" that Biscuit would be tempted to drag into the house. So, I still had to supervise Biscuit's nighttime trips to take care of business.

I grumpily trudged downstairs and opened the side door. Sniffing, Biscuit ran to the detached garage.

"Biscuit!" He disappeared around the corner. I realized that I must have left the garage open when I had returned in the golf cart earlier in the morning.

"Crap, and more crap!"

Biscuit had started to bark and wasn't stopping. With my luck, a raccoon had probably found the trash can in the garage. I cursed my responsibilities and my little dog. I loved him dearly, but he could be such a pain. I stuck my feet in some slippers and went outside.

Biscuit suddenly stopped barking. I halted, feeling the silence like an iron weight. Every scary movie I'd ever seen came rushing into my head. This is where you're supposed to run and call the police, not go off investigating on your own. It's the part in the movie where you scream at the extremely stupid girl, it's always a girl, in the movie that she shouldn't go in there.

I was indecisive, but my fear for Biscuit won out. I had to get my dog. Why was he quiet all of a sudden? I picked up the first thing I saw as I continued toward the garage. The rake was not a weapon, unless you wanted to sweep someone aside or stab them with a blunt wooden handle, but a garden tool was better than nothing.

I rounded the corner and entered the dark garage. I flipped on the light. Nothing. Great. I was starting to sweat as I imagined how I was about to die.

I called from the doorway, "Biscuit? Biscuit, come here. Now."

I felt more than heard movement in the shadows. Biscuit's head popped out from between the stacks of boxes. He was eating something.

"Yuck, Biscuit. What have you found?" Relieved that he was OK, I hoped he hadn't found a dead mouse.

Biscuit's palate didn't discriminate. I went to get him, then noticed that the moonlight shining through the window threw a shadow across the wall.

The perfect outline of a person's head.

I froze, and my intake of breath was audible. I raised the rake. As I did, Biscuit ran forward. Two hands came from behind me around my midsection, pinning my arms to my sides.

I started to scream and struggle as Biscuit proceeded to attack the leg of my captor. In my bedroom slippers, I attempted to kick him, but my soft, little shoes made ineffective, padded thumps against his shins.

"She's a fighter," said the voice behind my head. "I think she's going to be a better sparring partner than you."

I flung my head back trying to head butt my assailant. A pain shot through my head as I connected with his jaw. I thrilled at his string of curses and oaths.

The shadow materialized. The deep voice came

with a recognizable body. The instant I saw him, I felt stupid... why hadn't I been more alarmed by the pictures?

He narrowed his startling blue eyes and grimaced. "We weren't ready to meet you yet." The guy I had so stupidly examined as a curiosity earlier reached toward my face. I was sure he was going to hit me, but instead he set his wrist gently on my temple. I instantly felt a jolt like an electrical plug connecting with its socket. The rake fell from my grip and clattered onto the concrete floor.

"Sorry, Mia," he said evenly. I barely registered his deep voice.

Biscuit continued his attack, snarling and biting while I saw the world close from full view to a pinhole surrounded by black. Then...nothing.

***

I squinted as I opened one eye and then the other.

Someone had pulled the shades in the downstairs area, so I couldn't tell the time. I looked down to see why I couldn't move. Although I was in my dad's recliner, my hands had been taped together with what appeared to be duct tape. My ankles were also bound together. They hadn't bothered to tape my mouth, but maybe they had realized that we were out in the middle of nowhere. Who would I call for?

Even though I felt fortunate to be alive, I knew that I was in big trouble. I scanned the den for my cell phone.

"I took it."

I looked up to see blue eyes staring at me from a

chair pulled in from the dining room. "Took what?" I answered, startled because I didn't seen him at first.

"The cellular phone, the computer, whatever you're looking for..." he replied softly.

"So, what do you want with me?" I squirmed, suddenly aware that I was alone with him in my house and wore my short pj set that necessitated a robe even in front of my dad.

"I don't want anything," he answered enigmatically.

"Then leave me alone. Leave now, and I'll pretend I never saw you."

I was incensed at seeing Biscuit at his side. The guy had one hand stroking his little golden head. Biscuit looked content. My dog was such a traitor.

"You need money? My dad leaves some cash here for me. You can have it." I waited to see if Blue Eyes would take the bait. "But my dad will be back at any time, and you'll miss your chance." And for good measure I added,

"He carries a gun."

"No, he doesn't, and I don't think he'll be back any time soon."

"He'll be back sometime today," I stated with assurance.

A male voice came from around the corner. This guy must be the other one from the picture. The one who had grabbed me from behind in the garage.

"Good morning, our little fighter." He walked into the room. He smiled and sat down on my sofa.

Em was right when she had remarked about their looks. They were both exceptionally good-looking. Does that make it any nicer to be attacked and tied up? Nope. It proved that you can't judge a book by its cover. They didn't look like drug dealers or gangsters. They both looked like the kind of guy you wished would ask you out and never did.

The guy on the sofa was holding my laptop and looking at the screen. He began to read. "Mia, I got here and will talk to you tomorrow. It's going to be a long week, so if you need something, just e-mail. Remember that Mrs. Anderson is always there if there is an emergency. I may not call you if we work late nights.

Love, Dad."

"Oh, by the way, I'm Arizona. Your head butt gave me a bloody lip last night." He stated it without any malice and placed the laptop on the sofa. "And you are

Mia."

OK, how bright is the intruder when he gives you his name? Or maybe he plans on killing me, so it won't matter.

"Regulus thinks I was wrong to grab you last night, but I am a little impulsive sometimes." The guy with the blond hair was still smiling.

"Listen, I told your partner, Rejules—"
"Regulus...like Regulator," the blond said.

"OK, I told him that you could have the cash in the house and whatever, and I won't call the police. I want to live. I'm smart. You won't have any reason to hurt me."

"She certainly stays calm in a crisis," Arizona told his partner. "You're a real negotiator," he said to me. As if I needed a compliment. "We don't need your cash."

"I'm not sure what we're going to do with you," Regulus said from the corner of the room.

That comment scared me more than the other one's chitchat. I started to look around frantically for something to use as a weapon. Could I even defend myself with the duct tape restricting my movement? All I could see to get my hands on in the living room was a pile of remote controls and a heavy lamp. Perfect. And here I'd thought the rake had been pretty useless.

Regulus seemed to sense my increasing distress. "No one is getting killed today. No one is going to physically harm you."

"Is this some type of kidnapping head game?"

"I'd love to play some games with you," answered Arizona.

"You think I'd let you touch me?" I growled through my teeth as I felt anger winning out over panic.

"Don't flirt with her," Regulus snapped to Arizona. "You're scaring her."

The smile left Arizona's face, and he was serious when he looked at me next. "Accept my sincere apologies. I meant no offense. Umm, I think I'd like to eat something. I'll see what I can find in her kitchen."

I looked across at Regulus to see if he would be following Arizona to the kitchen, but he didn't move. We sat in silence as I wondered how I might escape. I could stand and probably hop to the door if they were out of the room. But then, where would I go? I couldn't drive like this, and we were too far out of town to walk anywhere.

I noticed the time on our grandfather clock for the first time since waking. I saw that I had missed the first tardy bell at school. I would be missed. Em would know something was up. Could I last that long? He was staring at me, but I ignored him. I closed my eyes and tried to think logically. While playing *Quest of Zion*, I had several strategies to turn the tide if losing a battle. I could throw my opponent by changing the location.

Chapter Four

Seeing is Believing

"I have to go to the bathroom," I said calmly.

"OK, we'll both go," Regulus answered.

"There is no way I can use the toilet with you in there with me."

"Why?" he asked.

"Are you crazy? I can't. You'll have to wait outside the door. But I gotta go."

Regulus pulled me out of the recliner, easily hoisting me into his arms. I stiffly avoided looking into his face as he carried me to the downstairs bathroom. It occurred to me that I could try to struggle or head butt him, but I scrapped that plan since I had no follow-up move.

He set me on my feet in front of the door. Since this bathroom was basically a powder room with only a sink and toilet, the cabinets lacked anything that could help me escape. He looked around once, then stepped out of the way to allow me to enter.

"Can you manage?" he asked.

"Yes," I hurriedly answered with my face turning red.

He stared at my wrists. "Here, be a smart girl. I'm doing this against my better judgment." He stuck his hand in his pocket and pulled out a metal object that promptly ejected a blade.

I sucked in air involuntarily.

"Hold out your hands, and I'll cut the tape," he said in a calm, slow voice as if speaking to a child.

I obeyed. Once he had cut the binding on my ankles as well, my mind began to whirl with the possibilities.

Regulus shut the door, and I could tell that he was still on the other side.

I reached over, turned the lock, and sat on the floor with my head on my knees. What did they want from me? I huddled there for a good half hour.

"You know you can't stay in the lavatory all day. I didn't see any tools. Just how long do you plan to stay in there?" Regulus sounded cranky.

I refused to answer. I was still hoping I could figure something out.

I could smell food. The blond guy had actually gone into my kitchen and cooked himself something. The nerve! I couldn't believe I was a prisoner in my own home. I listened and their voices turned to colors in my mind's eye, spreading a warm glow that I associated with good things. That didn't make sense. I smashed down the treacherous emotional glow of warm yellow he emitted and tried to concentrate on his words.

"Tell her, man," Arizona's cheerful voice came

across in a hushed whisper. "We could use her help."

I could make out every word if I pressed my ear against the door.

"She's not supposed to know yet," Regulus murmured.

I was getting panicked. What did he mean by "yet?"

"It's not time," Regulus said. "I can't risk her knowing too much. We could have walked out of there last night if you had followed the plan."

I sat leaning against the door and waited. I heard sniffling. I bent my head down and pressed my cheek on the cold tile floor to look under the door. Biscuit's wet black nose was wedged in the narrow space. He started to whine.

"Your little pet is becoming distressed," Regulus said.

"That's because he's scared."

He laughed. "Your little pet isn't scared in the least, and you shouldn't be either. If Arizona or I wanted to harm you, it would be done. We would have taken care of that last night. Actually we're your friends."

"Oh yeah," I muttered to myself. "My friends always drug me and get out the old duct tape. Favorite pastime."

I always know about people from the colors they exude from every pore. It's there whether I want to see it or not. I didn't know why their colors didn't warn me.

Why hadn't they done anything to me? I did concede that you never know about the crazy ones. I had watched movies where the kidnappers make you trust them.

"So, you guys on America's Most Wanted?"

"I don't know what that means." I recognized Regulus's voice.

In the silence after his answer, I could hear Arizona smacking away on whatever he had cooked. My stomach growled.

"You know, like you're wanted for some heinous crime in ten states and the FBI is looking for you. And you always wear a wife-beater tank." Except that's not how you look, I thought.

"Your FBI does not have information about me."

"Maybe she meant the CIA," said Arizona. I heard a pop as an object hit the floor. "Hey, you almost hit me with that."

"We are agents of the IIA." Regulus's voice was slow and probing, as if testing this piece of information.

"OK, real cute." I visualized my irritation rising like the red bar of a thermometer. I was getting irritated. I talked at the door. "Listen guys, this has been fun and all, but you will get caught. My friends know I should be at school today. My friends know about you."

"Do they?" Regulus asked. "Now that's a problem. Sorry, Mia. I had hoped that your friends wouldn't become involved."

But I wasn't listening to the last sentence. I heard the words, "Sorry, Mia," and I knew I had experienced a déjà vu moment.

I flashed back to the seconds in the garage last night when he had walked toward me. He had said my name last night. This creep knew my name before

Arizona had read my dad's e-mail. The gravity of this was sinking in like a heavy weight pressing on my chest. Had these guys been scoping out my house long enough to know my name? And why? What had they been planning to do to me and Dad?

At that moment, I heard a chime. My laptop sat on the living room sofa notifying me that someone wanted to chat. I guessed that the sound represented a message from Em. She probably wanted to gripe at me for not being at school.

I flattened to the floor and saw Regulus's shoes retreating. I figured that he was going to see about the sound in the living room. And there sat my cell phone on the floor. It must have fallen out of his pocket. I froze and held my breath. Could I somehow get my phone?

I quickly unlocked the door, opened it, and bent down to retrieve the phone.

"It's just the computer," I heard Regulus say. Footsteps started in my direction. I scooted back into the bathroom and closed the door, locking it. I fumbled to dial. In my haste, the phone fell and hit the tile floor, sliding across and behind the toilet. I clumsily dove to grab it.

"She has the phone," Regulus yelled to Arizona. He shook the door handle. "She'll call the police."

"We know about Pete. We know he's alive," Arizona said in an urgent voice.

I stopped breathing. I blinked and sat down on the cold tile, no longer reaching for the phone.

"Curse you, Arizona," Regulus's voice was a low growl. "You have chosen her fate."

***

I shivered and leaned back as I jerkily slid down the wall to sit. The pattern of roses on the bathroom wallpaper swirled and I forced myself to focus on the curling edge at the seam. The paper was coming unglued like my mind, I thought. Voices from the other side of the door grew louder. I started to wonder if I had hallucinated the entire day.

Or maybe the events were just one of those extremely vivid dreams. In a flash, I remembered the early days of Pete's disappearance when all of his friends were questioned. Those days, I'd walked around in a dreamlike state. No, a nightmare. The police, of course, had reassured us that there was no sign of a struggle, and therefore no reason to believe that Pete had been taken. Also, there was the fact that kidnapped teenagers didn't pack a duffle bag.

"Mia, answer me, or I'll bust the door in," came a persistent voice through the wooden barrier between us.

At first, only a squeak came out of my mouth when I tried to answer. The squeak exploded from me in an angry deluge. "You had better tell me what you know about Pete, and you had better tell me now. If this is some head game, you'll be sorry 'cause I am the wrong girl to mess with."

I clamped my hand over my mouth. What was I saying? These guys had information about Pete. And if I instigated their anger, they were less likely to tell me anything. I inhaled deeply, and then exhaled in small puffs.

"Calm down," replied the deep voice I now

recognized. Regulus sounded close, as though his face was only inches from the door. "I'm going to take the door off the hinges, or you can unlock it. I'm sure you want to talk to us about this."

I listened to Regulus's voice, so calm and reasonable, so disarming. Maybe his voice belied his growing anger. I knew he could get inside the bathroom easily enough. I just hated to lose that one last bit of control I had of the situation. He did have something I wanted, and he was well aware of it.

I'd waste time if my stubbornness forced him to remove the door. I didn't swing the door wide as that would probably have knocked me over given that I was restrained to small areas of movement. I peeked out, and Regulus stood with his arms folded, leaning against the door frame.

"I'm glad you opened the door." He opened it fully, stepped inside, and retrieved my cell phone from the floor. In the last few moments, I had completely forgotten about it. Now the cell phone didn't matter. What did matter was finding out if they knew something about my brother.

Arizona appeared out of nowhere with the duct tape and held it up to show Regulus. Then, he bent and began unrolling it.

I froze as he balanced on one knee to wind the duct tape around my ankles. In this close proximity to both Regulus and Arizona, I could see that they were both closer to my age than I had first thought. Being scared out of my wits had skewed my perception. I couldn't make an educated guess since all the guys I went to school with looked like teenagers with their stubbly chins and lanky limbs.

"I think we can do without the restraints, don't you?" Regulus asked.

Arizona stood a little close for comfort. I stumbled to move away and he backed out of my personal space. He smiled shyly.

"OK, let's give her some room," Regulus said as he nodded to Arizona. They both took a couple of slow steps back, never taking their eyes off me. I mimicked their slow movements. Though I wasn't taped, my arms and legs felt wooden and tense.

"Can we sit and talk without anyone doing something rash?" Regulus asked.

I led the way to the sofa, extending my hand like a gracious host. He sat on one end, and I picked the opposite edge. Arizona sat on the coffee table, which put him right between us, ignoring Regulus's glare. I edged away, disconcerted that I was within touching distance of both.

"Mia, sometimes things are not as they appear," Regulus said.

I had the uncanny feeling that he was talking to me the same way one talks to a mental patient. "What do you know about Pete?" I cut in, all business. I made an effort to sound calm and rational.

"The more important question is, what did Pete know?" Arizona said.

Regulus gave him one sharp look that instantly quieted him.

"OK, I'm not good with riddles. What did Pete know? What the heck does that mean? Was he in some kind of trouble?"

"Pete knew about us, and who we are," Regulus

said.

"So, who are you?"

"We are enforcers."

I could see Regulus and Arizona making steady eye contact with each other at this point, but I didn't have the faintest idea why. Did they expect me to say, "Ah, that makes it clear?" The silence was heavy. I heard the grandfather clock's pendulum swinging rhythmically in the hallway, weighing on my brain like a dark purple fog.

"We are unsure if Pete ever confided in you about the IIA." Regulus offered the words as if prompting for information.

"Is this some secret organization, like the Mafia or something?" I tried to tone down my mocking sarcasm. I wanted my answers about Pete. I knew my brother well enough to be quite certain that he wouldn't be involved with anything illegal.

Regulus nodded his head, appearing to have come to a decision. "IIA stands for Interdimensional Immigration Authorities. I think it would be better for us to show you something important to the IIA."

The statement filled me with dread. Is this something that Pete knew about? I swallowed audibly.

"OK."

Regulus rose, and Arizona jumped to his feet. They led the way outside to the front lawn, and I followed. The sun was shining directly overhead, so I knew it must be around noon. I was still in my short pajamas, but I had become unconcerned about this minor detail in the events of the morning. I did have the good sense to wear some tennis shoes as we left the house, and now I was glad as I tried to keep up with the two guys leading the way down my gravel drive.

Both Regulus and Arizona wore boots, so they walked like they were on an easy hike while I had a difficult time keeping up. The crunching sound filled my head, along with a visualization of the pictures I had taken with my cameras. And then I just went blank as I tried to keep up with their swift pace. The driveway had never been paved since it extended for a half mile, and I was fairly winded as we approached the end near the waiting booth. I still didn't see anything out of the ordinary when Regulus and Arizona started toward the spot opposite.

Buzzing began along with the tickle up my back. The instant Regulus's feet entered the swirled spot on the ground, he was gone. Literally. There one second and gone the next.

I gasped in shock. Arizona heard, turned his head toward me, and winked as he stepped into the flattened spot of brush.

I looked from side to side. I was alone.

My knees wobbled. I sat on the bench of the waiting booth. I blinked hard.

Once, my dad had taken my brother and me to a magic show in Branson, Missouri. The magician had walked on the stage and amazed us with a variety of tricks relying on sleight of hand and faith of audience. As a finale, he had made a helicopter disappear from the stage. We were thoroughly impressed.

This was another déjà vu moment. What had happened? It had to be a trick, of course. Not magic.

You don't just step onto a spot and disappear. But just as my imagination could not devise a place for the helicopter to be hidden from view, I couldn't imagine a hiding place for Regulus and Arizona. I walked over to examine the spot where they both had stood momentarily. I circled it and looked around to make sure that I was still alone. No abracadabra. Only me and the birds.

And the buzzing sound that seemed to engulf me. I flashed back to the moment that Regulus had disappeared.

I scooted my foot forward to the edge of the circle of flattened grass. I inched my toe into the circle. I don't know if I thought I would disappear to the mystical hiding place where Regulus and Arizona were surely waiting for me, but nothing happened. Nothing except for the vibration that buzzed through my head and traversed down my body like silver mercury trying to converge but instead, wiggling aimlessly.

I planted both feet in the circle and waited again. I closed my eyes expectantly.

I had definitely lost my grip on reality. A mental replay of the events of the last twenty-four hours flashed through my mind like a cartoon flip book. I went back to the bench and sat leaning my head back against the cool wood of the booth and closed my eyes.

I opened them, expecting to see Regulus and Arizona standing there. The blond, Arizona, would be smiling since he didn't seem to be able to wipe that constant grin off his face.

I was still alone.

I sat as the sun slid from an overhead position, and my stomach began to protest. When you aren't wearing a watch, time becomes meaningless, gauged only by the traveling sun. I couldn't tell if I had been there for thirty minutes or two hours.

I lay on the bench, looking up at the roof and noticed my camera. My camera held the proof. Tangible evidence that I wasn't out of my mind. I disengaged the tiny memory card and ran up the drive as gravel pierced my canvas sneakers.

The door was wide open. I could just hear my dad asking if I had been raised in a barn. I ran to my bedroom to insert the memory card into the computer. I chewed my thumbnail in anticipation while the computer seemed to take tortuous minutes to open the files for viewing. My hair, which had been pulled back into a neat ponytail before bedtime last night, hung in a wild tangle around my head. I tried to brush my fingers through the mess and get it out of my eyes.

The images displayed on the screen, and I rapidly clicked through the first ones. The camera had taken pictures during the night. I hit the arrow key furiously trying to move past the array of animals that the camera had recorded. Ironically, there were five times the number of pictures as the previous time I had checked the card.

"Apparently moon phases do make a difference in feeding patterns," I said, finding the humor in trying to get past those images.

I sucked in a breath as I displayed the picture I wanted.

I wasn't going to be committed to an asylum after

all. There on the screen stood Regulus and Arizona. You couldn't see their faces because they were both walking away from the camera when the motion detector activated. It caught them at the moment right before Arizona had turned and winked at me. I knew this because in the next moment, they were gone.

The next frame proved it. I looked closely at the leafy overhang of a tree, brush in the background, and a small clearing where I knew a flattened circle of grass pressed on the Earth.

Biscuit started barking about sixty seconds before the front door opened. I leaped out of my desk chair and ran down the stairs to meet the two guys who would surely laugh and explain the trick. At the bottom of the staircase stood Mrs. Anderson with her little old lady bag clutched firmly to her chest.

"Dear, you scared me half to death," she said in a trembling voice.

"Jeez, Mrs. Anderson, what the heck are you doing here?" I sounded harsher than I intended.

"Your daddy asked me to stop in and pick up the grocery list early this week," she answered. "What in tar hill are you doing home?"

She seemed to notice that I wasn't exactly dressed for school and still wore my pajamas. "Oh dear, are you ill?"

I gave a small, guilty smile. "I'm fine, Mrs. Anderson. I was a little sick this morning, but I'm fine now. Must've been just a woozy stomach. I was actually going to hop in the shower." A lie. The last thing I needed was to have Mrs. Anderson call my dad and tell him that something was wrong. And the truth was definitely out of the question.

"Honey, I'll just wait here until you get finished bathing." She smiled. I could see that she was determined to take care of me. My dad had insisted that Mrs. Anderson check on me often and run errands to keep our household operating in his absence. I barely restrained myself from rolling my eyes as I nodded in resignation.

I practically sprinted to grab some clothes as I made my way to the bathroom. I pressed my forehead to the door frame and peeked around just enough to peer downstairs, but Mrs. Anderson was nowhere to be seen. My mind was whirling with the possibility of Regulus and Arizona returning to talk to me while she puttered around. I was squeaky clean in record time, no singing, no messing around, or any of the usual pastimes I was accused of practicing in the shower.

I pulled my damp hair back in a ponytail and didn't take the time to dry it. My hair was still slightly more blond than brown from the summer sun these days, but my face was pale and my hair wet and dark at this moment, and I really did look sick. I pulled on some jeans and a T-shirt that stated "Self-Rescuing Princess" on the front. I didn't apply any makeup, but I thought maybe some pink lip gloss would bring some color back to my face. Mrs. Anderson was a sweet old lady, but she didn't understand that I didn't need mothering. I did very well on my own, thank you.

I leaped down each stair hoping that Mrs. Anderson would be finished with whatever she thought she needed to be doing. As I rounded the corner at the bottom, there she stood, wiping her hands on a kitchen towel.

"Sugar, no wonder you had a sour stomach, after eating that junk." She tutted. "I cleaned up the kitchen...what a mess. I warmed you a bowl of chicken broth. It's some of my homemade that I stored in your freezer last winter. I don't know what your daddy was thinking, letting you eat all that junk. You will feel like new after a bowl of my soup."

I nodded without answering since I knew she didn't require any conversation from me. I sat at the kitchen table and proceeded to scarf down the broth. It didn't take long for me to finish the bowl, and I actually did feel remarkably better after getting something in my stomach.

"Really, I'm totally fine, Mrs. Anderson. Please don't stay, or I'll feel guilty 'cause I know you were just dropping by for the list." I longed for her to get the hint.

"OK, dear, if you're sure. I do have an appointment at the beauty parlor in half an hour. I got the grocery list and will bring things by later in the week."

I set my hand on her elbow and guided her to the door. "Thank you so much," I cooed. "I just don't know what we'd do without you. I think I'll take a nap now, and I'll be like new tomorrow." I opened the door and gave her a quick hug.

She smiled as she tottered onto the front porch. "You have my number, and don't hesitate to call if you need me."

I stood on the porch as she walked out to her Lincoln, a tank of a car that seemed to swallow her behind the wheel. I stood in the doorway while it seemed that she took her sweet time to drive out at a three mile per hour pace.

As soon as the mammoth car was out of sight, I turned to reenter the house, but stopped as I heard footsteps. I looked up to see both Regulus and Arizona walking from around the corner.

I studied them suspiciously. "How did you do that? Where were you?"

"Mia, let's sit and talk." Regulus motioned at the wicker furniture on the front porch. He had shed his jacket, and I noticed his build for the first time. He had some ridiculous biceps. Not the kind that looked like he bounced at the local bar, but muscles that were proof of a physical training routine.

I wasn't scared. "I don't want to sit. I want answers, about you and about Pete." Sticking to my earlier line of questioning, I was unwilling to give up until they could tell me something about my brother.

Arizona gave me his coaxing smile I had seen often during this twenty-four hour period. "That's what we're here for. Answers."

Anybody would be blinded by the good looks of these two. Arizona seemed so harmless. Any girl my age would fall victim to his easygoing manner.

I sat in one wicker chair, while Regulus sat in the other. Our knees were almost touching, which made me slightly uncomfortable. Regulus looked a little agitated. His blue eyes narrowed as he sat straighter and pulled his chair back an inch. Arizona lounged sideways on the porch swing with one leg casually draped across the length of the seat.

"Arizona and I think you can help us. So, we're prepared to give you some answers."

"So, you came here for my help."

"Initially, no, but it seems that after talking about it, it might be wise."

"First, what do you know about Pete?" I noticed an almost imperceptible glance between the two.

"You need to understand about us before talking about Pete." Regulus twitched.

"OK, who are you, and what's with the disappearing act? You were there one minute, and nowhere the next."

"Disappearing act is a good description. We didn't cease to exist, we just changed our existence to another plane."

"Is that, like, magician talk?" I fought to avoid a sarcastic tone.

"We entered what you might call a dimensional doorway," Regulus answered, sounding casual, "and were in our world."

I stared at them both. Either I was crazy, because I had actually witnessed this unexplainable event, or they were.

Chapter Five

The IIA

"Oh, is that all?" I said in a deadpan tone. "I thought you did something really cool."

"I'm serious, Mia. I know it's hard to believe. And you saw it yourself," Regulus said.

"Hard to believe doesn't even scratch the surface. It's just not possible. I don't believe in the Easter bunny, and I don't believe in doorways that make you disappear."

"We are assigned to your area." Regulus glanced at Arizona, still quiet.

"What does that mean, assigned?"

"This area is our responsibility. We monitor your woods for unauthorized immigration."

"So, how does this door work? You didn't ask anybody to beam you up..." I nodded my head and widened my eyes in mock seriousness.

Regulus looked at me, his brow lowered in

confusion.

Arizona chortled. "She's making a joke. She is such a funny girl." He pushed at my shoulder lightly to emphasize that we were buddies. It's difficult not to like someone who laughs at all your jokes. Arizona was certainly starved for humor if he thought my sarcasm was that funny.

"I don't understand," Regulus said. His irritation sliced through the air. "You shouldn't know how the door works. You have no reason to know anything more than necessary. Trust me."

I wanted to trust him. His colors of warm yellow gold told me that he was good. But I couldn't tell Regulus that he had a good aura any more than I'd tell Austin that his was good, too. I relaxed and focused on the conversation.

"Trust you, huh? So, you leave the starship to monitor my driveway for immigrants. And you take them back to outer space with you when you find them?" I was positive he didn't have a clue about my starship reference. I knew my remark was a mean retaliation to his high and mighty dismissal of my need to know more.

Regulus's humorless eyes narrowed. "You also don't need to know what happens to dimension immigrants. I think your government calls it a zero tolerance policy for certain crimes."

"My government. So you work for whoever is on the other side of the door. And who is that?"

Arizona had stopped grinning. "We have already explained that we are bound to the IIA. No joking, Mia."

"Then why do you seem so, I don't know..." I

hesitated, searching for the right word. "Earthly, if I'm supposed to believe this?" "Because we're human, like you," Regulus answered. "We've also been trained for this assignment. My purpose has always been to monitor the portals. Arizona's birth was in your world. Now he is of the IIA."

"Oh, I'm so relieved that you weren't going to tell me that you're aliens or *Men in Black*. Although that would make about as much sense as this." I slumped down in exhaustion. This had seemed like the longest day of my life.

"Who are the Men in Black, Mia? Should we be aware of them?" Regulus continued to frown and his blue eyes glittered. He was as tense as a turkey on Thanksgiving.

Arizona hooted louder than before, thoroughly enjoying every minute of our interaction. He leaned toward me, smoothing his longish blond hair off his face. "You should know that he's always like this…so serious."

Regulus waved his hand as if to indicate that Men in Black reference was of little importance. "We think that you can lead us to the criminal who is aiding the immigrants in entering Earth."

"For argument's sake, let's pretend that I believe this. Why on Earth would I care if these immigrants decide to live here?"

"Because the immigrants in Whispering Woods will destroy the human population."

At this truly inopportune time in the conversation, I heard a vehicle coming up the drive. The motor was loud, indicating that the rumbling wasn't Mrs. Anderson again. I saw Austin in his Jeep.

"Don't leave." I was panicking as I looked around for a hiding place. "I need to know about Pete and what he has to do with all this. In here." I grabbed Regulus's hand as he was closest to me. He flinched automatically, as if the touch of my hand had burned him. His gaze darted to our hands and up to my face when I tugged.

Both of them followed me quickly as I led the way toward the same downstairs bathroom I had locked myself in earlier this morning. The ironic twist of the situation didn't escape me.

It had only taken moments for Austin to appear on the other side of the screen door.

"Austin, what in the heck are you doing here?" I looked through the screen door.

He grabbed the door handle. "You gonna ask me in?"

"Why bother? You usually just let yourself in."

Austin clutched his chest, then grabbed the shaft of a make-believe arrow to remove it from his heart. He steadied himself dramatically before opening the door. "Emily sent me a text earlier saying that you didn't show at school today and wouldn't answer her chat. She was major textually frustrated." He flung his head to the side to move his black hair out of his eyes.

"So?"

"You had pictures of the so-called ax murderers from the cam, remember? I was coming over here to go all
Chuck Norris on them."

"You crack me up," I said glibly. "I told you that I wasn't even worried about it."

"You should be. You should be more careful. You had the front door open, and your alarm's not even set, is it?" He pointedly looked at the unit on the wall beside the door.

"Mrs. Anderson just left," I lied. It alarmed me that I was lying so easily when I considered myself a fairly honest person.

"So, you and Mrs. A just hangin' out today?"

"No, I was sick."

Austin pressed his hand to my forehead.

I backed away. "I might be contagious. Sicker than a dog all morning. You wouldn't even want to go near the bathroom. Been in there for hours." I was babbling, and I knew it. If Austin didn't want to back off, telling him I'd been barfing this morning might just do it.

"OK, OK. I get the picture. No need for the details. I can hang around if you need me," he said with no enthusiasm.

I gave a feeble laugh and shook my head. "I'll be fine. I just need to get some sleep. And please text Em that I'm fine, and I'll talk to you both later."

"Sure." He turned toward the door, pointed at me, and then to the security alarm keypad.

His college schedule left him way too much free time.

He stopped with his hand on the door. "Lock up behind me, all right? I know you aren't worried about people near your house, but I am. And Em is." He brushed his long dark bangs aside to make sure we were making eye contact.

Guilt's heavy hand sat on my conscience. "Alarm on... the minute I shut the door," I said. "My dad has nothing to worry about with you around."

Austin left, pulling the door shut. I parted the blinds enough to see him jump into the Jeep and leave.

Exhaling in relief, I turned directly into Regulus's chest. "Yikes! Don't sneak up on me." My voice was as high and squeaky as a five-year-old's.

"Good job, Mia. Does your boyfriend visit you unannounced often?" Regulus asked.

"He's not my boyfriend."

"So this boy who isn't your boyfriend... He knows about us somehow? And this Em person knows also?"

"And he's not a boy. He's probably the same age as you." I felt somewhat defensive of Austin. I had forgotten that they could hear every word. Regulus and Arizona didn't know about the pictures. My friends were becoming involved in this craziness...that bothered me.

"I have a camera set up taking pictures at the waiting booth." My words came out sounding breathy. He was waiting for more explanation.

"Waiting booth?"

"The red wooden bench by the road." "And this camera took our picture," Regulus said. "Does anyone else know?"

"No. Just Austin and Emily."

Regulus frowned. He did a lot of that after hearing anything I had to say. "Do you think that they will tell anyone else?"

"Definitely not." I shook my head adamantly to emphasize that I was positive that everything I had said was our secret.

Regulus still frowned and lifted his eyebrows toward Arizona who had made himself comfortable on the sofa. He was looking through a magazine on the coffee table with his feet propped on the edge.

"How are you so certain of this?" Regulus's blue eyes drilled into me.

"I know my friends." My voice had taken on a pleading tone. I took a breath since I wanted to sound confident and sure. "My friends will cover for me no matter what. My dad would freak out, and he wouldn't leave me alone or even let me leave the house if he thought there were people lurking around in the woods."

"Ah," Regulus nodded, but the perpetual frown was still there. "Let's agree that this must remain our secret."

"So, tell me where Pete is."

Arizona stopped flipping through the magazine and focused on the conversation. He looked from Regulus to me and back. "We don't know where Peter Antares Taylor is located," Arizona said. "But he should be the one helping us instead of you."

I stood gaping in astonishment. Pete had hated that middle name. When we were little, he had threatened my life if I were to ever disclose it. They did know something about Pete.

"So, what do you know? You obviously know something." I stared at Arizona since he was actually telling me the things I wanted to know. I couldn't hold back the excitement in my voice.

"Peter was supposed to join the IIA, and he disappeared." He shrugged as if that were the end of the story.

I knew there had to be more. "What?" I couldn't fathom how Pete would think about leaving Whispering Woods, because that's what it meant to me. Pete had been planning to leave.

"He disappeared," Arizona said again.

"Yes, I heard that part." I bit my tongue in frustration. Be nice. The voice in my head tempered my impatience.

"He was to join the IIA and something went wrong," Arizona continued.

"Pete wasn't old enough to join any IIA or whatever you call yourselves," I answered in stubborn denial. "He was a teenager, like me."

"Peter was a man," Regulus said. "He was eighteen, right?"

I crossed my arms over my chest, hugging myself. "He was still in school. He was too young."

"We're close in age to your brother. The IIA begins training agents as young as possible. Your brother would be a strong and valuable agent."

"We would like to locate him as much as you do. Maybe if you help us, we could help you," Arizona was not looking at me, but at Regulus.

I measured what Arizona had said. I looked at his open, friendly face that told me to trust him. Regulus, on the other hand, had suddenly grown quiet. And he was avoiding eye contact. They say that sometimes it's what a person doesn't say as much as what he does say. I wondered what was left unsaid. Were they telling me only what they thought I wanted to hear?

Regulus turned toward me, and his eyes met mine briefly before he went to the window to gaze at the woods. "So, you will assist us." His tone told me that he had made a decision, not that he was asking for my help. Was he ordering me?

***

I don't know what I expected, but I didn't expect the ordinary. After Regulus and Arizona explained that there was a portal in my woods, I envisioned the two would demonstrate a scientific phenomenon by exiting via dimensional doorway. Of course, I was disappointed. Shortly after obtaining my agreement to aid them in stopping the immigrants, they both left me sitting in my living room wondering about the reality of all the things I took for granted in my normal life. I wanted to fully interrogate them on the details of their lives. Could it be true that such things existed in the world?

After they left, Mrs. Anderson called to ask me repeatedly if I was feeling better. I assured her that I felt fine and all was well with me and the world. I tried to concentrate on things I should worry about.

Normal things.

I looked at the clock and remembered that I had an appointment after school with Dr. Bleeker at the local

U. Dr. Bleeker had volunteered to be the mentor for my senior science project. I was lucky to get him. It didn't matter to me that the real goal was to recruit the seniors of Whispering Woods High. Not only did Dr. Bleeker have a great reputation, but he wasn't as stuffy as the other professors.

I could catch up on a day of classes, but I couldn't

miss this appointment. I grabbed a jacket and raced out the door with my research logbook. My dad had handed down his car to me over the summer so I could drive to school and run errands. Last year, I had always ridden to school with Austin. Now that Austin didn't attend Whispering Woods High, I was on my own for a ride.

***

I knocked on the office door and waited patiently.

"Come on in, Miss Taylor. I was just finishing up." Dr. Bleeker opened the door wide and returned to his computer. I followed behind him and sat in the chair directly in front of his messy desk, which was covered with folders, a fuzzy red stress ball, and a Star Wars pencil holder. I leaned forward to look at a Bart Simpson bobble head.

"I have a collection of my favorites."

I smiled at the plastic figure. You just can't help but like a bobble head. "Here's my logbook," I said as I handed the thin black book across the desk.

"Tell me about it, Mia. I'd rather talk than read through a bunch of boring entries." He tossed the book onto a corner of the desk away from most of the clutter.

"Yes, sir. What would you like to know, Dr. Bleeker?"

"No need for formalities, Mia. I insist. Call me Eli."

I was stunned at the request. I had never called a teacher by his first name. Much less a college professor. I didn't know what to say.

"Now, tell me what steps you have completed and if your observations to date have surprised you." He removed his narrow glasses and sat back in his office chair, which reclined to an amazing degree. His voice evoked a pleasant gold swirl around my brain.

"I have my cameras mounted and recording activity in areas around my house. I go and collect the memory cards every day, check them and write down what I see."

"Do you get activity in all locations?"

"Pretty much. I was really surprised at first."

"So, a lot goes on in the woods when we aren't looking." He nodded with an interested look.

You don't know the half of it, I thought. "Just lots of deer and raccoons."

"And you wrote that your chosen method for measurement of the vegetation harvested will be the number of animals eating your plots times the minutes spanned on record. You'll then chart that raw score for increasing intensity with the changing moon phases."

I was impressed that he remembered the details of my project. I had told my dad the whole project scenario half a dozen times, and I doubted that he could have recited a summary that efficiently. I tried to remember if he was mentoring any other students from my class. No wonder Austin had said I was lucky to get him.

"That's it. And I have all that in my log." I indicated my proof by looking pointedly at the logbook.

"And you're keeping the camera images in an electronic folder on your computer, I presume?" Dr. Bleeker's tone was the same, but his words threw a blanket of dark green caution over my mind.

I ignored it. "Of course." I thought about the pictures I needed to remove before an outsider could view them. The fact that he mentioned the images freaked me out. Was I getting paranoid?

"You'll need to print out some of those to mount onto your project display board."

"Oh yeah, right." I sighed in relief.

"And I recommend that you start entering the data into a spreadsheet. That will make it easy to chart the results."

"Wow. I never thought of that. Great idea." "That's why I'm here."

We sat in comfortable silence for a minute.

"So, how do you like Whispering Woods?"

A strange question, plus the shift in topics threw me off. I took a minute to gather my thoughts. "I've lived here all my life."

"I'm just trying to get to know you better. I like to get to know the students I work with."

"I like Whispering Woods a lot. I'll probably go to college here." I presumed this was the real question he was asking.

"That surprises me. We don't recruit as many from the local schools as we should. Kids are ready to get out. See the world." He motioned a hand toward the picture on his desk. "My two will probably attend college as far away from here as possible. They think Whispering Woods is boring." In the photo, two young boys held hands with their mother leaning over them. "Not me. I'm happy right here."

"That's great to hear. Maybe I can give you a tour of the campus while we're working together."

"Sure, Dr. Bleeker." I just wasn't going to be able to call him Eli.

I looked at my watch. I had already been in his office for much longer than I had anticipated. Squirming in my seat, I hoped he could tell that I was ready to leave.

"That's all we need to discuss today. Next time, why don't we meet at the student center for a soda? You can see a little more of the campus that way. Would you like to come by next Monday after school for our meeting?"

I straightened and nodded. Dr. Bleeker handed the slim logbook to me. I had forgotten about it. "That would be great. Thank you for your help, Dr. Bleeker."

"E-mail some of your images. I'd like to see your evidence."

"Sure," I said. I was glad I didn't have anything with me today.

"I just had a thought. Why don't I walk you out and show you where my lab is located? If you ever come by and I'm not in my office, you need to check there.

Sometimes I let the time get away from me."

"Oh, OK." I looked around as I followed him down the hallway and through an exterior door. I walked swiftly to keep up with Dr. Bleeker's long strides.

Although the campus was located on the outskirts of a small town, students at Whispering Woods University didn't have to leave for anything. Private donations had ensured that every academic and social necessity was more than adequately provided for the students. The architecture of the buildings gave the onlooker the illusion that the entire campus had been built in the 1800s. This old-world illusion coupled with the fact that the buildings were nestled in the Ozark Mountains created a beautiful campus.

We left the cobbled sidewalk and entered the nearest building. I looked at the oil paintings of what I assumed were former professors lining the walls. Because I wasn't paying attention, I almost missed Dr. Bleeker darting into an open doorway.

"Here is where I am most of the time when I don't have classes scheduled," he said.

I looked around at the test tubes and equipment. It looked like a medical lab. There were even refrigerated cases lining the back wall, full of more test tubes.

"What do you do in here when you don't have class?"

Not being a science person, I couldn't imagine how someone would spend extra time in here.

He laughed. The deep chuckle rumbled in my ears. "I have some research that I'm interested in. Contrary to what you may think about overworked professors with heavy class loads, I actually have a lot of free time."

"Cool," I said, because I didn't know what to say. I had never heard a teacher say that they had free time. Dr. Bleeker really was different. "Yes, it's pretty cool," he said with a large smile.

"I'll see you next Monday then." I exited Dr. Bleeker's lab and headed toward my car. I had been at the appointment for an hour and wondered when I would talk to Regulus and Arizona next. Would they contact me? Was I supposed to contact them? I still had a hard time swallowing the whole concept of a portal in my woods. Or as they called it, a dimensional doorway. Did they live here or on the other side? How did they get through? I had stepped on the same spot as Regulus and Arizona, but I obviously still resided here.

I paced myself in driving home. The last thing I needed was for the town patrol car to pull me over for speeding. I finally arrived at the entrance to my driveway. I turned and proceeded at a snail's pace, searching the woods on both sides of the drive. Nothing. I ridiculed myself, wondering if I expected to see Regulus and Arizona seated in my red waiting booth in anticipation of my return. I continued up the drive, looking here and there for any signs of life and was disappointed.

I grabbed my logbook and stepped out of the car. I looked at the stacks of boxes that lined the garage and could visualize seeing Biscuit's head peek out from them less than twenty-four hours earlier. Why had Regulus and Arizona been in here in the first place? Had they been hiding in wait for me? That couldn't be right, because I was certain that Regulus hadn't intended to involve me. I had far too many unanswered questions.

I could hear Biscuit's bark as he generally thinks he is a guard dog. I skipped up the steps to let myself in, turned off the alarm, and let Biscuit out for a potty break. I looked around the house to make sure that I was alone. Yep. No one but me and Biscuit.

I remembered that I had turned off my cell phone while I was with Dr. Bleeker, so I powered it back on and looked at the display. Jeez! Em had sent me ten text messages. I had to give it to her for persistence.

I had Em on speed dial. "Em, it's me."

"What's going on with you? You OK?" Em's voice was always urgent and important. Hearing it raised a vision of sticky pink bubble gum in my mind.

"Did Austin let you know that I was sick today?"

"Sure, but you usually still text me." I heard a little petulance in her voice because I had talked to Austin and not her.

"True, but I didn't want to miss my first appointment with Dr. Bleeker, so I had to go to the campus and take care of that."

"Oh."

It didn't make sense to me that I was the one who was supposedly sick today, but here I was, trying to soothe Emily's feelings because I hadn't texted her back. This is why guys made better buddies than girls.

"Wanna come over and do homework?" I asked.

"Sorry, can't. I have to watch my sister in a recital tonight." Her voice had pepped up at my invitation. "Maybe I can hang in Zion tonight, though. Gotta go now, my mom wants me to be ready in ten minutes."

"Bye, Em," I said before she ended the connection. I stared at my cell and wondered what it would be like to live at Em's house. Em's family consisted of two siblings, both parents, and a set of grandparents right next door. They ate dinner every night at exactly six. The menu for all the home-cooked meals could be found on the fridge door. A calendar of family activities was even posted for frequent viewing.

I peeled the cellophane wrapper from the edge of

my frozen dinner.

Chapter Six

Regulus

Rule number one: Do not engage in personal relationships with subjects in your area of assignment. All emotions may be cauterized in cases of extreme deviance from the regulations set forth by the IIA.

Regulus recited the lines in his head until he had a difficult time listening to Arizona talk. Arizona talked more than anyone he had ever known.

Regulus grimaced while reading the contents of Mia

Carina Taylor's genome file. He could understand why the IIA wanted her. He transmitted the final file onto his electronic reader with a flick of his wrist. Carrying it to the bottom bunk bed, he attempted to lie on his back and stretch out, but his feet hung off the end. He bent his knees in acknowledgment of the futility.

The only light in the dorm room was a desk lamp shining onto paperwork strewn across the desk. Neither Regulus nor Arizona had read the numerous pamphlets left by the dorm mother, a woman of generous physical proportions and advice.

"No alcohol, no noise after quiet hours, no parties." She had said the words in a booming voice. "Sign here that you understand and agree."

She hadn't given them time to read the contract but looked around the tidy room suspiciously. Then she had tossed the pamphlets on the bare desk and left.

"The logical person here would be one with access to a variety of resources, someone who blends in easily, someone who hasn't lived here since birth. It has to be someone from this university."

"Yes, we've already agreed on this." Regulus mumbled the response as he stopped reading.

"Then we should use whatever resources Mia may have. It's the only way that we will find the immigrants that are hidden in this town. We are running out of time. If they are allowed into society and breed, the genetic pool is ruined. Can't let Whispering Woods turn into a cesspool." Arizona laughed and leaned over the edge of the bed to look down at Regulus. "And the girl...she's easy. She's already cooperating fully."

"We don't need her. She's a risk." Regulus rubbed his temple. He looked at the digital clock that was given to incoming freshmen at Whispering Woods University, or Whispering U as they heard it called. 11:15, the orange numbers glowed. He wondered if the girl, Mia, was alone or if her father would be in their home. Would she be asleep? Or maybe she would be with the one that was called Austin.

"Did you hear me?" Arizona said. "I said that spending some time with Mia is better than most of the assignments we get. She's a funny, attractive—"

"You will leave her alone." Despite himself, his words came out in a deadly, slow hiss. He changed his tone and offered an impersonal, flat spiel. "The IIA has marked her. Since Peter is absent, she is next. She's to be our third. Our gatekeeper."

Silence. The digital clock clicked as the numbers changed and changed again.

"You're attracted to the girl, aren't you?" Arizona spoke the words in a low voice, his respect evident. Regulus didn't answer.

Arizona dropped his head back onto his pillow. He shook his head in disbelief. "Don't worry. No one will ever know."

"You're imagining things. My restraint is beyond your comprehension. Your non-disciplined early years make it hard for you to understand." Regulus continued using a flat voice.

"You don't believe that, Regulus. We're the same. The IIA can train you to suppress and channel your emotions. But they can't erase them." Arizona stared up at the dirty ceiling above his head.

Regulus rubbed both hands over his face. His voice was low and barely audible when he spoke. "Yes, they would just erase me."

Chapter Seven

School Daze

After I went to bed, I found myself looking at the clock every five minutes. 9:00 p.m., then 9:05 p.m., 9:10 p.m. ... Eventually I kicked my legs in frustration. I was exhausted from lack of sleep, but I couldn't stop myself from looking at the clock.

I jumped out of the bed. Biscuit, for once, didn't move from the rumpled blankets near the foot. I looked at his sleeping figure in envy. At least one of us would get some sleep.

Grabbing my jacket and shoes, I padded barefoot down the stairs. The house was dark with only a nightlight shining at the end of the stairs. I disabled the alarm and opened the front door to see a star-filled sky. I finished dressing while standing on the porch.

I knew that I had to go down to the waiting booth. I had walked the drive so many times that I could do it with my eyes closed. I took a flashlight on my way out, but knew that I didn't need it. The stars glittered en masse, a glow that would make the flashlight appear blinding and harsh. I quietly slipped through the grass at the edge instead of using the crunchy gravel surface to announce my journey.

When I reached my destination, I sat in the waiting booth and drew my knees up to my chest. My long pajamas clung to my warm skin in the autumn night. I leaned back and looked up at the twinkling lights and remembered the last time I had studied the night sky. Dad, Pete, and I had camped in a tent in the back yard and built a bonfire. I looked up, lost in happy memories of toasted marshmallows and bad jokes.

I closed my eyes trying to see my brother's face. He'd disappeared only a couple of years ago, and I was relieved that I could still remember him clearly. People said that we looked alike, and I could see the similarities in his brown eyes and the wave of his dark blond hair.

I dreamed that I heard their voices. Regulus and Arizona were talking in hushed tones. Then arms encircled my body and I became weightless. I was rocked in the most comforting rhythm.

***

I awoke to the harsh light of morning and the insistent beep of my cell alarm. Biscuit licked my face with the enthusiasm that only a dog can have at seven in the morning. I sat up confused. I wasn't sure what was real and what I'd dreamed. My flashlight lay on the nightstand table. A note had been left on top.

***

Morning people have always gotten on my nerves. First period English buzzed with the sound of voices recounting escapades true or imagined. I call it talking smack. They were supposed to be working on group assignments. I didn't care about the project but needed quiet to start the week. Some silence to clear my head and think, but my team members were the loudest group of individuals who have ever walked the planet.

I tried to concentrate on Angel Lester, who dominated the conversation with her descriptive who's who from the party on Saturday night. Angel's fast talking washed over me in a dark blue persistent wave of information.

Lucky for me, Em was assigned to the same group. "Are you even listening to me, Mia?" She waved her hand in front of my face in an exasperated motion.

"Uh, yeah, sure I am." My eyes traveled up the wall to the clock and back to her face.

I noticed that Em had worn her hair in a side ponytail. Was this what she had been talking about? She seemed to be on the eternal quest for that look, that *America's Next Top Model* look.

"What did I just say?"

"OK, I wasn't listening to the last thing you said." I smiled sheepishly and nibbled on my barely there thumbnail.

Em's iridescent bead bracelets sparkled as she straightened them on her wrist. "Girl, you have been in your own world for the entire period." She paused dramatically. "Something is going on with you. It's Austin, isn't it?" She leaned forward in anticipation with her head cocked closer to mine in a plea for confidence.

I rolled my eyes. First my dad, and now Em thought that something had to be going on with me and Austin. I fervently wished my dad hadn't teased Emily the other day about it.

"Class, go back to your individual seats now for journal entries on your teamwork," Mrs. Cranford said in a high, lilting voice. Students groaned. Mrs. Cranford smiled gleefully from her perch on a bar stool at the front of the room. I smiled back, glad for the solidness of her expectations. Mrs. Cranford, in her crisp pink Oxford button-down could always be counted on for schedules and order. Saved by Mrs. Cranford.

Back in my seat, I proceeded to arrange my black paperback journal in front of me. I wedged my fingers into the pocket of my tight jeans to retrieve the neatly folded note. Discreetly unfolding the paper, I hid it in the center of my open journal. The words on the page were tidy and small, moving in a straight line, not sprawling like mine on the paper beneath it. Each letter appeared to me in a different color even though I knew the note was written in only black ink. Only weird synesthetes like me see in Technicolor.

Mia, I order you to stay out of the woods at night.

There are dangerous travelers who would see you harmed.

We will talk again tonight.
—*Regulus*
I stared at the words with a renewed sense of chagrin. I had been in those woods all my life and never been scared or worried. The woods were a safe place for me. And I just added the words I order you to my list of pet peeves. Maybe there was something about the woods that would lead me to Pete. I read the note for the tenth time.

The rest of the school day was about as exciting as watching paint dry. I've read somewhere that people can do things on autopilot, like driving. You begin at starting point A and somehow end up at point B without ever realizing that you made the journey. It's a form of self-hypnosis. I was too new at driving to imagine that yet. School was a different story. I ended at point B in last period and couldn't tell you about any classes I attended.

The clock eventually struck 3:00 p.m. and the bell filled my entire being with anticipation. I chewed the edge of my thumbnail as I walked as fast as possible to the parking lot. My mission was accomplished as I jumped in the driver's seat and pulled out ahead of the string of cars exiting the lot.

My eyes darted to the speedometer, and I exhaled, pressing the gas pedal to increase my speed. I prayed that Deputy Sorrel wouldn't be sitting in some hidden spot waiting on speeders.

My mailbox at the end of our road finally appeared.

My stomach tingled, and I slowed for the turn.

The gravel crunched beneath the tires as the car slowed to a lumbering crawl. I pressed the button to roll down the window when I came to the wooden structure at the side of the driveway. With the car in park, the fresh air rushed into the car, tinged with a warm scent that filled my head with orange and yellow.

This is ridiculous, I scolded myself. Did I think that I would see Regulus and Arizona waiting for me to return from school? I shook my head in self-disgust. Shifting the car into drive, I slowly made my way toward the house. My eyes flicked up to the rear view mirror, more out of habit than necessity.

And I saw something.

My foot slid off the accelerator as my head jerked around. I hadn't imagined it. I caught my breath as a tall, pencil-thin dark figure stood near the waiting booth. By tall, I mean to say, inhumanly tall, not Michael Jordan tall. The figure had been as still as a statue, but how had I missed it the first time?

It started to move toward me, and the car jerked to a stop. Not because I had slammed on the brakes. Nope. I had forgotten all about driving. I had hit a tree planted inconveniently at the side of the drive.

The damage wouldn't be much, but I was frantically trying to get the gear shifted into reverse. I pressed hard on the accelerator pedal. The motor roared. The car wasn't moving. I looked into the mirror. The tall figure was now much closer and still moving at a steady pace. My heart pounded and my throat seemed to contract on its own.

I looked down and saw "N" marked next to the gear shift. I shifted into reverse. My foot was heavy on the pedal, and I almost took the car all the way back to the figure. Don't panic, I whimpered to myself. I made the mistake of looking in the mirror and felt a silent scream rising in my throat. If I had ever imagined what the Grim Reaper might look like, he had just materialized in my driveway. No, he didn't carry a scythe, but he was actually wearing a black robe of some sort. His face was a shadow in the hooded shroud of dark material that he wore.

A mechanical, high-pitched whining sound and then a piercing whistle sliced through the air. The figure made eye contact with me in the mirror and next crashed onto the back of my car. His previously covered face now pressed into the back windshield and squeaked as it smudged an oily streak vertically down the glass.

I heard screaming. After a minute I realized that the hair-raising shriek was my own. The piercing cry was the same scream I had used when Pete had accidentally, or on purpose—when you have a brother, it's hard to tell —shot a bottle rocket into the back of my tennis shoe when I was ten years old.

The car door opened, and I was still screaming as Regulus hauled me out of the car. He shook me. Not a gentle shake of waking someone from a night's sleep, but a hard jerk meant to snap me out of my terror. It did the trick. I stopped screaming. Maybe I should be glad that he didn't slap me out of my hysteria.

My knees started to buckle, and Regulus wrapped his arm around my back to lift me to a standing position. "What do you think you're doing?" he asked.

I looked at him in confusion. "What am I doing? What am I doing? Minding my own business. Coming home from school. What the heck was that? Was that a man?" The words tumbled out in a rush as my adrenaline picked up again.

I took a deep breath and peered around Regulus to see Arizona dragging the figure by the arms toward the road.

"We thought you were trying to run over it with your vehicle," Regulus said with a grimace.

"Uh, no...just trying to get away." I moved his arm away and leaned against the car for support.

"You were going the wrong direction," he said with a slight upturn at the corner of his mouth.

"Um, yes, Captain Obvious, I got a little panicked and...and... Never mind." Arizona neared the area where I had recently watched them both disappear into thin air. Two motorcycles lay sideways on the grass nearby.

"Is it dead?" I tried to still the tremor in my voice.

Regulus seemed so calm and unaffected by the whole situation. "No, we don't execute, unless necessary."

"So, what stopped him and what's Arizona doing?"

"He's tagging him and sending him on to be processed," Regulus said.

"Tag him? He's not a deer or some game." My voice lowered in wonder. "What is he...it...doing here? Did he come from the doorway?"

Regulus shrugged. "One of many unauthorized travelers in your woods."

Arizona pulled out a silver device. He pressed the box to the temple of the inert figure in black.

"No, stop!" I shouted. Why, I didn't know.

Arizona's eyes met mine from across the drive. He

shook his head in answer before pressing a button on the metal cylinder he held. I was accustomed to seeing a smiling almost flirtatious look on Arizona's face, but now his smile seemed evil. He pulled the body a couple of inches toward him, stepped back, and disappeared.

I stared at the spot where Arizona and his captive had vanished. Even though I had already seen this same trick once before, it dumbfounded me. I turned to Regulus, who just happened to be watching me looking as though he was interested in my reaction.

"This is all just blowing my mind." I felt my legs quivering with the consistency of well-chilled Jell-O.

He walked over to lean against the hood of my car. My eyes traveled to the dent from hitting the tree. I guess I was lucky that the bumper was the only part that had been damaged. What if that thing had gotten to me? What had it wanted?

"OK, Mia, ask questions if it will settle your mind to have answers."

"The thing that Arizona tagged, man or not?" I started with the question that I had already asked once.

"Human species," he said. "But not of this Earth."

"He looked like he was more than seven feet tall," I stated.

Regulus nodded.

"When you say not from Earth, what planet?"

"What planet?" He shook his head. "Listen to me, Mia. I said that he was not of this Earth. There are many dimensions that inhabit the Earth."

I knew I was frowning. I started to chew on my thumbnail. Had I missed the science lesson on dimensions? I remembered studying about Jupiter and Pluto. Dimensions, not so much. I was feeling stupid when Regulus started to laugh. My mouth dropped open as I was stunned by the oddity of that sound in relation to his normal demeanor.

"You're not supposed to know about the others. We work hard to keep your people unaware." Regulus had certainly been entertained by my dumbfounded expression.

He was still smiling.

And with the swiftness of a dark cloud blocking the sun, his smile was gone.

"I apologize for this incident. I underestimated the resources held by other entities." Regulus avoided my eyes. "I didn't think others would know about your involvement with the IIA."

"Involvement?" I know my mouth dropped in disbelief. "I'm not involved. I only said I would help you to get information about Pete and you know it."

"Mia, you are now associated with me and that aligns you with the IIA. Whether you want to be involved or not." Regulus finally made eye contact.

I shook my head, trying to negate his statement. "So was the man from the doorway trying to hurt me?"

"Yes, he planned to remove your presence from the portal." Regulus spoke as if he were running down his to-do list for the day. Get supplies, check; see what Mia is up to, check; stop dimension traveler from killing Mia, check.

I tried to remain calm and inhaled deeply. I had been through worse before.

When my mother had decided to abandon ship, I

was a small girl. Pete wasn't much older and certainly not able to handle the responsibility of a younger sister. My dad had checked out mentally for two long months. He'd paid the bills and brought home groceries, but the house held the air of a family recovering from a natural disaster. Survivors. I imagine that the unearthly quiet in our house was similar to the lack of conversation after a natural disaster like that tornado that had touched down in Whispering Woods the same year. People just don't have anything to say afterward.

My dad didn't talk much until Aunt Candy called and offered to let us live with her. She'd thought Pete and I needed a real home with two parents. That's the day that my dad mentally came back to life. The tongue-lashing he had given my aunt convinced her to never call again.

"Is he the only one or will there be more?" I asked Regulus.

I registered the look of surprise on his face. Did he think I was going to fall apart? Cry?

"There will always be more. For now, there's a certain organization that wants to remove you."

"You mean kill. Why do you say remove, like it isn't personal? They want to kill me."

"Remove, kill, it's the same. And it isn't personal.

It's a strategy to win. They just don't know that the IIA always wins." Regulus said the last sentence with absolute certainty.

"So, who is trying to kill me? I refuse to call him tall, scary guy."

"In general, they're Slips. They enter this dimension to escape life in their dimension. The IIA doesn't permit it. These Slips carry a deadly disease that would be fatal to the population of your Earth."

A loud rapping noise clapped through the air and Regulus shoved me toward the ground. I tasted dirt as he proceeded to not-so-gently press the back of my head.

"Ow, watch it."

His fingers dug into my hair, and he lay beside me on the ground, placing a single finger to my lips to signal the need for silence. I could feel the tension in the weight of his arm across my back and he eased his hand from the back of my head. I stared into his eyes trying to read an explanation of the severity of the situation. Regulus lay still and calm as if he did this every day.

I attempted to peer around his head and under the car to see if someone held a gun on the opposite side.

Raised voices and a scuffling sound ensued. Where silence blanketed the woods before, chaos had materialized.

"Uster," a voice growled. "Uster..." the voice moaned in a slow, drawn out plea.

I could now see the two pairs of feet. A moment later, a figure crumpled to the ground.

"It's clear," I heard Arizona report. A hand, his hand, reached down and took what appeared to be a weapon from the hand of the fallen person who could be a twin to the one who had come through earlier. I saw no blood and couldn't detect how Arizona had stopped him.

Arizona squatted down and peered at us underneath the car. "I knew there'd be another. This one would have taken you out. Shooting in blanket pattern..." said Arizona in disgust before he was interrupted.

A wailing sound emitted from a shroud of cloth that tumbled from the arms of the body on the ground.

"For crying out loud, I don't need this," he grumbled as he walked over to the bundle of cloth and pulled aside one edge to reveal a small, irate infant. The tiny face was red and had begun to scream in earnest.

I jumped to my feet, running over to Arizona and the baby. "No, no, no!" I stumbled over, knocking Arizona aside. The weapon fell from his hand, and I grabbed it and a clump of grass as well. I knelt on the ground while one arm shielded the small bundle.

The weapon in my hand shook only slightly as I pointed it at Arizona. I glared at both of them. "Over my dead body."

Chapter Eight

Slips

The dull metallic square I held didn't resemble a gun, but I knew the box was a weapon from the way Arizona had used it. It sat awkwardly in my palm, rectangular and heavy.

The infant lay in a bundle, quieted momentarily by the touch of my hand on its chest. I didn't know any more about holding a baby than holding a weapon, so I left it on the ground.

Arizona raised his hands in surrender. "Hey now, calm down, no one is going to hurt the infant." His eyes left mine for a second as he glanced at Regulus, who stood at my back.

Arizona approached and sharp pain seared my upper arm. Regulus.

He dug his thumb into my inner arm and the move worked as though he had pushed a magic button. My fingers sprang open and the weapon fell to the ground. I pressed my lips together to stop from crying out in pain. He kicked the metallic box a few feet away.

"Never...do...that...again." He said each word through gritted teeth. "Too unpredictable. Stupid girl."

Arizona bent to retrieve the bundled infant. He looked into my eyes and smiled reassuringly while removing my hand I had placed protectively on the baby.

"Mia, I won't harm this one. Trust me. I haven't harmed anyone today. Only incapacitated both intruders." Arizona's eyes pled, as though willing me to believe him.

"What are you going to do to them?"

I glanced at the adult body lying on the ground, seemingly unconscious and maybe even dead.

"They both must return to their world. Consequences will follow, but that's not for us to deliver. What do you think you can do for this infant, Mia?" He watched me rub my right arm where Regulus had so effectively applied pressure. It still smarted, and a red mark was left where Regulus's fingers had been.

"But it's a baby, Arizona. Defenseless," I whimpered. "I just didn't want you to hurt it."

"Enough talk. It is our duty," said Regulus, cutting into our conversation. "Taking it back through."

Regulus picked up the baby and tucked it into the crook of his arm, the way you'd hold a paper bag of groceries. The camaraderie I had felt earlier with him had gone.

"I'll come back for the other one," he said, not even

turning to face us while walking toward the portal. As he passed the body on the ground, he casually rolled it over with the tip of his boot and appeared to confirm that it was alive. Then, he resumed his pace, carrying the baby like a football and stepped into nothingness.

"So, how does he just step, presto, through the portal? I step there and nothing happens." I rubbed my arm, looking at Arizona for an explanation.

He sat down beside me on the ground and tentatively took my hand. I started to pull back out of his hold when he forced my fingers over his wrist. Guiding my index finger and rubbing it lightly over the area below the meaty part of his palm, he traced the flat shape of an object beneath his skin.

"What is that?" I felt goose bumps crop up on my arms.

"Sensor chips," Arizona said.

"And the chips control the portal?" "It signals more than controls," he explained. "There are many dimensional entities who know how to control the portal. And of course, the IIA controls them as well."

"So, there's more than one portal?"

"Of course. Hundreds across this dimension of your Earth." Arizona motioned toward the area near the waiting booth. "This portal has been rarely used until the last couple of years. Regulus and I were assigned to this area a year ago."

I did a mental calculation. That would be around the time that Pete had disappeared. An idea was blossoming in the back of my mind. "Did Pete go through the portal?"

"No, we're quite sure he didn't."

I held my gaze steady and shielded my emotions so he couldn't see my disappointment. Going through the portal would be the last thing I wanted for Pete. Just finding him here, in this dimension, was going to be hard enough.

"Did you know Pete?" My voice sounded low and small. Desperate.

"No, but I'd like to meet him." I noticed his use of the present tense, which reassured me. I found it hard to dislike Arizona as he was always smiling and so darn friendly. Though I'd threatened him with a weapon in the past hour, he didn't seem to hold it against me.

Out of the corner of my eye, I saw Regulus walking toward us, minus the baby bundle. He avoided my eyes. I guessed he would be holding a grudge over recent events.

"I'll take this one, too." Regulus used the same device Arizona had on the first Slip. When the "tagging" was completed, he grabbed both arms of the figure on the ground. Arizona rose to help Regulus move the Slip a few yards. Then Regulus disappeared with the body in tow.

"Do you have some more food in your kitchen? I'm so hungry. I could eat a pony."

"Eat a horse. You mean eat a horse, right?" I tried not to smile, but the corners of my mouth lifted.

"I was just trying to use your slang phrases." He looked embarrassed.

"Oh, I wasn't making fun of you." I straightened out my smile into a serious face.

"Yes, you actually were, but it's because we are friends, right?"

I tried to read him. Was he trying to gain my trust, or did he think that friendships were gained in a day or two?

"If you can get me to Pete, you're my new best friend," I said as sincerely as possible to remind him of my goal.

"If I were you, I wouldn't point a weapon at me or at Regulus again. You're on our side in this. I'm patient. Regulus is not."

I nodded my head in understanding. What had just happened had been a reflex. I didn't plan to do it. I certainly wasn't thinking about choosing sides.

"Mia, you and me, we're the same, but...Regulus is different. He won't understand your compassion."

"We're the same?" I cocked my head and raised an eyebrow. "And just how is that?"

"You and I are both from this dimension. Two peas in a pod."

I stared at him.

"Peas in a pod. I said it the correct way, didn't I?" Arizona said.

"Sure, Arizona. But I doubt we're from the same pod.

I gotta hear how you figure that."

"Can we eat while we talk?" Arizona grabbed his stomach in mock expression of dire hunger.

"Will Regulus come back and wonder where we've gone?"

"He'll know. We track each other automatically."

Arizona flipped his hand up in a gesture to show me the implanted chip he had revealed earlier. He did this in the way I might hold up my cell while saying my dad could reach me anywhere.

My mind was on overload with trying to process the information Arizona was giving me, so I let that one drop. We drove the rest of the way to the house. As soon as we entered, Biscuit greeted us. I felt bad for making him wait so long to be let out for a break. My dad had built a small fence around a section of the backyard for Biscuit to be able to run off some energy. He ran the perimeter, barking at a lone squirrel that had decided to hang out in a tree on the west side of the fence.

"Tell me how we are two peas," I said as I shoved a large frozen pizza in the oven.

We bent in unison to pick up the small pieces of sausage that had rolled off the pizza. He smiled and allowed me to grab them.

"What?" He grinned.

I thought about how Emily would be swooning over that face. "You know, you said we were 'two peas in pod.' How do you figure that?" I turned to scan the fridge for something to drink. I handed him a can of soda.

He popped the top and guzzled the orange drink. "My father worked for the IIA. My mother worked for Target in Phoenix."

"Really? You mean Target, as in the store?" He nodded to assure me that I had heard him right. "How does that happen?" I asked.

"It's not supposed to happen. My parents broke the rules of interaction."

"So do they live in Phoenix now?" I clicked the oven light on and peered through the spotted, filmy window to see that the cheese was not even melted.

"They're both gone." Arizona shrugged. "I lived

with my mother until I was four. She died, I lived in foster homes, and then my father came to get me."

"I'm sorry. About your parents."

"I'm fine. I've lived without either one for a long time."

I could tell he didn't want any pity. I answered the same way when people found out that my mom had left me and my brother. "Oh. Do you have more family?"

"The IIA." He went to the oven and bent to gaze through its cloudy glass window. "That smells delicious." He reached for the handle.

I pushed his hand aside with my oven-mitted one. "I've got it."

Looking up, I saw Regulus through the glass top of the kitchen door, which led outside. I don't know how long he had been standing there, but I did notice the strange look on his face. I felt the urge to explain what we were doing. Geez. This was the same feeling as when my dad had caught me doing something wrong. Like I wasn't supposed to have fun talking to Arizona.

"Come in." I waved my hand, directing him inside.

Regulus hesitated but entered, sitting in the nearest chair. He looked at the drink glasses arranged catty-cornered at the opposite end of the table. His eyes met mine. I felt a black cloud descend on the room.

"Arizona doesn't have time for this."

"What? You guys don't eat?" I remembered to check the pizza, which was probably on the brink of becoming a hard, sixteen-inch disk. I took the pizza from the oven and put it onto a large cutting board.

"There's plenty for all of us."

"Where was the first Slip when you came home in your car today?" Regulus glanced down at the plate I laid in front of him.

"You saw where. On my driveway."

I passed Arizona a plate of the hot pizza. I could see him salivating. He shoved the slice into his mouth and took a bite. I laughed when he opened his mouth to air cool the piece that had seared his tongue.

"He wasn't hiding?" Regulus asked.

"Nope. He was standing by the waiting booth, you know, the covered bench, when I drove past it. Then he started walking toward me." I eyed Regulus suspiciously. "I thought that you said in the note to expect somebody in the woods. Why the twenty questions all of a sudden?"

"It's too soon. I've calculated the odds of discovery, and it's monumental. Someone told them to send a scout ahead. I have a theory." He paused as if for effect. "Your friends are informers." He lifted the pizza slice to his mouth without taking his eyes from me.

"Are you crazy? My friends don't know anything. That is ridiculous. And even if I had told them something, Austin and Emily would never tell anyone."

"Really? You're certain of this?" Regulus asked between bites of pizza.

I glanced over at Arizona for moral support. I felt like I was defending myself and my friends, and I didn't like it one little bit. Arizona was taking smaller bites now and chewing each one to keep himself busy, I thought. He remained silent, his eyes flicking from Regulus to me.

"But they do know about me and Arizona in your woods. You told me that they saw the pictures," Regulus said.

"Uh...well...yes. They just think that you're two goons trespassing in my woods. Like maybe, you're thieves or something. Come on, guys." I looked from one to the other. "They're just ordinary people, like me." I laughed nervously.

"Like you? Mia, you are far from ordinary." Regulus shook his head and reached across to help himself to another slice of pizza.

Normally, I'd have said "thanks for the compliment," maybe blush a little in awkwardness, then move on to the next topic. But this time, there was just such gravity to the statement. And Arizona refused to meet my eyes while Regulus couldn't seem to take his off me.

"I have a feeling this is supposed to mean something to me." I fidgeted and started picking olives from my slice of pizza, unsuccessfully trying not to look at Regulus.

"Maybe or maybe not. I had assumed you didn't know anything, but maybe you know more about your situation than you have led us to believe." Regulus's squinted eyes told me what he thought.

"Don't have a clue what you're hinting at." I decided to keep eye contact with him because I wanted it to be clear that I was being up front. I found this task harder than it sounded. I'd discovered that Regulus was the king of the stare down.

Biscuit scratched at the back door, and I let him in. He wagged his tail with unlimited energy, gleeful to see his buddies back in the house. He chose to sit beside Regulus on alert in case any toppings happened to jump off his pizza slice. Biscuit was out of luck.

Regulus chewed slowly, meticulously, watching my reaction to every word he said. "So, you and Pete weren't as close as you let on."

"You don't know a thing about me and Pete," I said. "If Pete had a secret, he didn't tell me because he couldn't." I hated that Regulus filled my head with doubts about my brother. What had been going on?

"Not everyone can work for the IIA. Pete could and you can." Arizona said. I guessed he was getting as tired of the cat-and-mouse dialogue as I was.

"OK, I give. Why me and Pete, and not the average Joe? Why you and Regulus? Oh, I know, we're like superheroes, right? I should tell you now that I refuse to wear a cape." I shook my head while smiling.

Arizona's mouth twitched, but he was trying to be serious. "Your genetic makeup is special. Like Pete, you have a neurological gift."

"Oh yeah. I am a real brainiac. I can't even play along with *Jeopardy*. Guys, you have hit the wrong household for recruiting the Mensa squad." I didn't think I was dumb, but I sure knew my latest ACT score, and MIT wouldn't be knocking on my door.

Regulus grabbed a pencil and pad from the counter. *Oh great, he's going to give me a math problem or ask me to perform some other neuro-gymnastics.*

He drew a twisted rope on the pad. Cool. I could do *Pictionary*. "See this double helix? The DNA coding strand holds the genetic pattern that would—"

"I dreaded something on this piece of paper that involved math, but this may actually be worse. I should have paid more attention is science class."

Arizona laughed and held up his hand. "Stop, stop.

Summary, Regulus, summary."

"She is not an idiot, Arizona." Regulus ripped the sheet of paper from the pad and tossed the crumpled ball into the trash bin. The more Arizona laughed, the angrier Regulus seemed to become.

"Regulus, just tell me. What is this gift I have so inconveniently never discovered?"

"You are a synesthete, and so is Pete." Regulus looked at me expectantly for some kind of reaction.

"You're crazy if you think that's a gift. It just means my senses get crossed. It drives me nuts. How did you find out that I am? I mean, Pete got tested at the university, but I've never told anyone."

Arizona cocked his head to one side, the confusion clearly written on his face. "Why wouldn't you want anyone to know, Mia?"

"Because it's weird and different. And Pete hated it that teachers had that info in his student file."

Regulus looked as confused as Arizona over my reasoning.

"Your neurological gift allows your brain to combine senses and feel the natural portals of your world. There is nothingness in the portals, and you feel it," Regulus said.

OK, that last statement about "feeling nothingness" was about as contradictory as a statement could get. I stared at the front of Regulus's T-shirt. Anything was better than looking into his questioning eyes, which clearly expected me to say something.

"How would you know I can feel anything? I would have noticed this, right?" I had a flashback to the last two times in the flattened circle of grass that was the portal for Regulus and Arizona. The last time I was there, it had felt reminiscent of the first huge drop at the top of a roller coaster peak. I had been thinking I would do some disappearing act, so I tied my feelings to anticipation. The time before that I had gotten nauseous. So, I could feel a portal. No big deal.

"The IIA has your genome file as well as Pete's," Regulus said. "They recognize how you can use your gift.

So you've been officially recruited as an enforcer."

"OK, I get it. You guys are like those army recruiters that came to my school and tried to tell us how great it would be to serve in the military. Right? There is a problem here in that I don't want to join.

I'm still in high school, guys. I have a college plan. Get real," I said reasonably.

"You want to find Pete, right?" Regulus said with just enough threat.

The ringing of the phone prevented me from making a smart-aleck remark to him as I rose to answer it. I was sure that it must be a telemarketer, because the house phone never rang anymore. If anyone needed to call me, they just called my cell.

Or my friends would send me a text for that matter. That thought made me realize that I hadn't checked my cell in a while.

"Hello," I answered, tucking the handset into the crook of my shoulder and chin.

"Mia Taylor, please." The deep voice on the other end exuded authority.

"And who may I ask is calling?" I guessed a telemarketer, which was why I had told my dad that we didn't need a landline. The only person who called besides telemarketers was Mrs. Anderson. She called the landline because she wouldn't call my cell phone. When I asked her once why she never called it, she answered that she didn't have a "cellular phone" so she was pretty sure it wouldn't work. I remember thinking that was hilarious.

"This is Eli Bleeker," the voice on the other end said.

"Oh, hi Dr. Bleeker." I waited, wondering why my mentor was calling my home phone.

"We have a contract, umm, agreement that you're supposed to e-mail me on a daily basis concerning the status of the science project. Most of the time, I'm not that much of a stickler about the rules, but we've just gotten started and you haven't responded to my e-mails. I thought maybe I had written down the wrong e-mail address or that you're having Internet problems."

"Oh, gosh, I'm so sorry. I've been so busy with this being my senior year and all. I promise I will check in by e-mail today." I twisted the phone cord around my fingers and peered around the corner to see Arizona investigating the contents of my refrigerator while Regulus looked at photos on the top freezer door.

"Sure, I understand. I was just checking to make sure that we are on track. A mentor has a job, too," Dr. Bleeker said, and I could tell by his voice he was smiling.

I started to sweat when I saw Regulus remove the picture of Joey Blue and me at the spring dance last year. I was a good four inches taller than Joey in the picture and hated the outfit I'd worn. I silently cursed Em for talking me into wearing a dress and heels.

"Thanks so much for calling, Dr. Bleeker. I have to go. I'm cooking something in the kitchen, and I think it's on fire." My statement came out rushed and nervous.

"Oh, definitely, don't want to keep you. Come by my office at the end of the week for our face-to-face."

"Sure thing. 'Bye." I ran and grabbed the picture out of Regulus's hand. I slapped the four-by-six photo face down on the kitchen counter. Biscuit scratched on the back door, so I turned to open the door and let him out.

A loud crash and a thump sounded behind me the second I had my back turned on my visitors.

Austin lay splayed on the floor with one arm outstretched as if reaching for something to grab and the other twisted behind his back. The right side of his face was pressed against the floor, and his hair hung forward over the left side. Regulus's knee was lodged firmly in the square of Austin's back as he held the twisted forearm in place.

Startled, I turned and tried to form words that

would defuse the situation as my mouth formed a small "o." At least no one is bleeding, I thought optimistically. I saw Arizona poised conveniently a foot away to assist if necessary. Clearly, Regulus didn't need help. He wasn't even breathing hard.

"This," I said slowly, "is my best friend, Austin."

I guess I had thought that Regulus would be embarrassed at attacking my friend. He'd hop up and release Austin from the hold and shake hands or slap him on the back in camaraderie. But he didn't.

"Can you let go of him." This was not a question.

Regulus released the hold on Austin's arm and stood gracefully. He backed up a foot in the small space between the kitchen table and the sink. I saw that two glasses had been knocked over in the scuffle while I was out of the room. Now I knew how teachers must feel. I had only turned my back for a few seconds, and...

Austin rose with as much dignity as possible and followed my gaze to take in the pizza and the dishes that said I had not been eating alone. I guessed he hadn't previously noticed that detail.

"What's up here, Mia?" Austin said, refusing to look at Regulus or Arizona. He sounded as accusing as a husband who returned to find his wife cheating.

"Just eating pizza, as you can see." I tried to sound nonchalant, like I had guys Austin didn't know in my house all the time. I caught myself shifting from foot to foot and about to chew on my thumbnail when I stopped my fidgeting.

Austin standing near Regulus formed a stark contrast of man and boy. Although Austin was in college, he still had the tall, lanky frame that said he was still making that physical transition into adulthood. Regulus had taken off his jacket at some point, and his T-shirt clung to every muscle on his chest. I didn't think I was the only one who noticed his muscles.

This was not going to be easy to explain.

"I was worried about you not answering your cell and then I came to check and I heard guys talking inside your house. Since your dad isn't home, I came in to see if you're OK. The front door was even unlocked," said Austin as if he'd completely explained why he had gotten into a fight with someone inside my home.

"Oh." I glanced from Regulus to Arizona in a plea for help. What could I say about them that wouldn't give them away? I had a feeling all of this was top secret, and I wouldn't even know where to start with an explanation. "Hey Austin, these are the guys from my outdoor camera," would probably end badly.

Arizona stuck out his hand to Austin. "Hey man, nice to meet you. My friends call me Arizona. I'm an old friend of Pete's." Arizona's easy smile and outstretched hand forced Austin to play nice. How could anybody doubt that smile?

Nevertheless, Austin stared at Arizona's hand for what seemed a full minute before shaking it. If I'd been his mother, I'd have swatted him. But I wasn't and he had already been in jeopardy of appearing less manly while on the floor.

"Huh," Austin grunted. I had never seen him be so unfriendly. "How did you know Pete?" Austin wasn't buying it. He definitely had reason since Whispering

Woods was so small.

"He was in our guild. On *Quest of Zion*. He wasn't that active, but he was there." Arizona was still smiling despite the frosty handshake and questions.

I stared at Arizona trying to read his face. How in the heck did he know about *Quest of Zion*? Either he was an excellent liar with great insider intelligence or he gamed online. The first choice seemed less strange. I couldn't have fabricated a better explanation.

I could see Austin mentally measuring Arizona. Austin looked at me for answers. "These are the two from the pictures we looked at," he said.

"Sure they are," I said, processing the fact that he had recognized them. I gulped and tried to think of something to say. I knew that I looked nervous and guilty.

Arizona came to the rescue. "Regulus and I both started classes at the U this year, but we used to play Quest with Pete a few years ago. We thought we'd look him up since I had his home address."

Austin grabbed the back of a chair, swung it around, and sat. His arms rested on the back of the chair and he looked completely at home in my kitchen. He'd sat in my kitchen hundreds of times and looked the same, but I could see that this time he meant to establish his belonging.

"So, when was the last time you talked to Pete?" Austin's question held loads of suspicion.

"Really couldn't say. It's been a while. Couple of years I'd say."

"I know everyone from our guild in Quest. What's your username?"

"Blade Runner," Arizona said.

Austin's reception changed from one of wariness to extreme interest. Blade Runner was at the top of the high scores, mostly because he was the only character to ever solo the wandering boss, the black knight of the descent. He is also the only player who ever found the auto-life exploit, allowing him to keep control of his character even after hitting zero health.

If you can think about a businessman closing a deal on a statement, then that's what Arizona did with Austin in that second. Austin was all ears.

"Cool," said Austin nodding his head. "Why did you guys drive here in the middle of the night? And you're on motorcycles, right?"

"Yeah, when we got here and saw how late it was, we didn't think anyone was home. I called Mia and talked with her about knowing Pete, and she told us to come on out."

"She should have called me to be here. Her dad would keel over if he knew she had let two strangers into the house." Austin's reproachful tone was clearly meant for me as opposed to Arizona.

"Yes, we didn't know she was alone out here. It's too dangerous for a girl her age to be left home alone," Regulus said.

I was bristling as they talked about me as if I weren't standing right there. "Hello guys, standing right here, ya know. I have been making it just fine, home alone. I am fully capable of taking care of myself." I began picking up the drinking glasses lying on the table in small pools of orange soda. I grabbed a hand towel to wipe up the mess. How did this story that Arizona had somehow made up, spur of the moment, end up with me defending myself as a sane, responsible adult?

"Mia, we will be leaving now." Regulus eased toward the door.

"Oh, you don't have to leave just because Austin's here." I was afraid that they would disappear again and I would still be lacking all the answers I needed.

"I would like to take you out for dinner tomorrow night," Regulus stated.

My mouth hung open. I could tell I was no more surprised than Arizona or Austin.

"I can't go out on dates without my dad being here and without his permission." I cleared my throat in embarrassment. I knew this was just pretend in order to set up a meeting, but I was shocked at the thought of a date. I had dated a couple of boys in the last year. But they were just that.

Boys.

Regulus was not a boy. And he was from some other dimension. And he didn't even like me. It made me stop breathing just to think about it.

"I meant that Arizona would be there also, of course. Are you allowed to meet friends for dinner on a weeknight?" Regulus asked.

"Sure," I managed to answer. I scribbled on a scrap of paper. "Here's my cell number. Just give me a call after school tomorrow, OK? You have a cell, right?"

Austin looked surly while Regulus said, "I will call you tomorrow."

I nodded and watched Regulus go to the front door with Arizona following.

Walking at a leisurely pace, they let themselves

out and headed toward a motorcycle that Regulus must have ridden to the house earlier. Arizona sat behind Regulus, and they roared away down the drive.

Austin turned to me, glaring. "I don't like the thought of you having those dudes here alone. You should have called me. You know I could be here in minutes."

I rolled my eyes as I went into the den. Austin followed. I sat on the sofa and picked up the TV remote, trying to find something to distract from the current conversation.

"For that matter, you shouldn't be going anywhere with them tomorrow night unless I'm there, too." He still sounded as though he was scolding me.

"Austin, you're not my father, and I can go out with friends for dinner any time I like."

He sat beside me with his leg touching mine. I scooted over an inch.

"I think I need to see if I can find them online. See if their story checks out." "Not necessary," I said with an edge in my voice.

"And that guy Regulus wanted to take you out alone. He just included Arizona when you said you couldn't go on a date." He reached for my chin and forced me to make eye contact.

I hated it when he did that. "He did not. I just misunderstood him, that's all." I was reliving my embarrassment all over again.

"He's too old for you." The phone rang again. I ran to answer it.

"Where are you? I have called your cell a zillion times and it goes straight to voicemail." Emily's voice sounded extremely loud and demanding over the phone.

I turned down the volume. "Yeah, yeah. My cell is dead, and I need to charge it. We are way too connected. It does not mean I'm dead when I don't answer my cell." "Oh," she said in a small, tight voice.

I heard a little of the pink leave her voice and I immediately regretted my words. "Talk to Em while I find my cell." I handed the phone to Austin and searched for my cell phone and charger. They were in my car where I must have left it. I took a minute to look again at my dented bumper—the one that had hit the tree—and decided that my dad might not even notice the dent.

When I returned, Austin handed the phone back to me.

"So, you have a date or dinner or something with the hunky guys from the pictures." Emily was back to her normal voice and talking so fast I could barely understand her. "How do you get a date with both of them? Which one do you have the hots for, the blond or the dark-headed one? What are their names? Spill!"

I glared at Austin. He had pulled out a small pocketknife and was doing something to his fingernails. He was completely ignoring me. I gave up on the glaring and tried to concentrate on Em. I was not a good liar, and now I had to come up with some details that Emily would surely be asking. One lie just seemed to lead to another. I felt like a snowball gaining speed, rolling down Mount Everest. There was no stopping it.

Chapter Nine

Date

After school on Wednesday, I set my cell phone ringer on the loudest ring tone, a Lady Gaga song that Austin had downloaded without my permission. Charged fully the night before, the phone display revealed at least half a battery charge. It would have been a full charge if not for Em's insane persistence. She had not restrained herself from sending approximately thirty text messages during the day, between second and last period. Every time the phone had vibrated, I cringed at the thought that my phone would be confiscated and held in the principal's office.

I was exhausted from her endless questions. We only had two classes together this year, but she had utilized her time with me to the fullest extent by quizzing me nonstop. My lack of answers just seemed to make her more persistent.

Of course, the questions she had were far from anything Austin had asked when he had the full attention of Regulus and Arizona the previous night. Emily's questions were more of the descriptive variety rather than stuff that really mattered. What did Regulus have on? How tall are both of them? Don't you think Arizona looks like a young Brad Pitt? Her questions annoyed me. The questions were ridiculous, and I could barely answer without sounding irritated. I swear she was a breath away from asking to come see for herself.

At school, I thought a lot about how easily Arizona had lied to Austin. The lies had slipped off his tongue like a worn tennis shoe on a wet, mossy rock. If he could lie that easily, how was I to believe the things he had told me?

So, here I was, finally making my escape by exiting the parking lot, forced to stop and go, stop and go, behind a truck sporting oversize tires. I could see Em rushing toward the parking lot trying to stop me. I knew she wanted to talk some more, but I pretended not to see her. Emily had been a great friend through thick and thin, but this wasn't something I could easily share with her. I didn't like the lies, but how do you tell your best friend that you were having a close encounter of the third kind?

The drive from school to my house was the longest twenty minutes in history. I stopped in my regular spot outside of the garage. This part of our house tended to be more of a storage area than one meant to shelter cars. Biscuit greeted me with his usual abandon, tail erect and twirling in tight circles.

While I did my chores, I wondered where Regulus

and Arizona might take me to dinner.

I stared into my closet as if seeing it for the first time. Normally, I would reach in, grab a pair of my favorite jeans and a cute shirt. Yes, I would forego a T-shirt since Regulus had sounded so formal when he talked about dinner. It didn't sound like he was talking about a corn dog and fries. But in looking at my choices for something to wear, I groaned at the limited display of what normally passed for acceptable school grubs. It's not as though this was a date...

Not a date. Really not a date. Nothing resembling a date because three people don't go on dates.

I finally decided that I might try the casual dress that I had bought last year with Em. Actually, Em's mom bought it for me. A dress. Like I would ever wear it. But here I was standing in my room looking at a closetful of T-shirts. I frowned as I gave in and peeled off my jeans to change. I stepped into the dress, stuck my arms in the matching cardigan, and twirled in front of the long mirror attached to the back of my bedroom door. I grabbed the only shoes I had that weren't tennis shoes or boots. I never wore the flat, ballerina shoes anywhere, but I had to admit that they were kind of cute. Ugh. I looked like one of those preppy girls at school.

My phone buzzed to indicate a text message, and I wondered what Em could be asking me about now. I looked at the message, expecting to see another of Em's questions about tonight. I read the words. "Waiting outside. Regulus."

I gripped my phone and shook it in frustration. Why, oh why, would he do this? I was a second away from changing out of the dress. After my thirty second meltdown I realized that he had just sent me a text as opposed to calling. I had never imagined that he would know how to text. It just seemed disconcerting that the guy from another dimension blended so well in my teenage world.

I looked in the mirror again. OK, I didn't look like a total dork. And while my hands were definitely sweaty and tingly, I even looked normal.

I needed to get a life that involved more than hanging out with Austin and Emily online.

I could see two figures through the sheer curtain in the front oval glass of the door. Quit being nervous.

It's just a meal.

I yanked open the door and shrank back when Regulus's eyes widened. He squinted a lot in his suspicious study of a person, but now he was definitely not squinting. His eyes started at my head and traveled down to stop at the dusky pink flats. He didn't smile or nod approvingly, or say, "Hey, you look nice." He just stared.

It took Arizona a minute to open his mouth to utter, "N-ice, Mia." He drew out the first word so it came out in two syllables.

Heat crept up my neck to my face and ears. I saw that both Regulus and Arizona looked as they always did.

I was so overdressed.

"You appear to be ready," said Regulus, clearing his throat at the end of the statement.

"Yes, I am." I played it cool. "I had to dress up for something at school today and didn't have time to change or anything. I hope this is all right."

"Not a problem," Arizona said in his usual cheerful tone. He glided around Regulus to offer his arm to me,

"Off we go, then."

I shoved my hand in the crook of his arm. Um... awkward. This wasn't the homecoming court walk down the football field. Arizona grinned at me and then turned to smile fully at Regulus. I felt a little better in my dress after he did that.

We walked down the front porch steps and I noticed their parked motorcycles. I must have been so wrapped up in what I was going to wear that I hadn't heard the sound of them riding up.

I pictured myself straddling a motorcycle in my dress. The full skirt would allow me to swing my leg across the seat, but I would feel extremely unladylike. "Umm, I can drive my car." At both their blank faces, I waved my hand down the front of my dress to remind them of the problem.

"Your car won't work for this." Regulus swung a leg over to seat himself on the first motorcycle.

Em would be so into this. She would think she had died and gone to cool heaven. I shook my head at the thought and glared at him. Could he not give me a break? I already felt ridiculous.

"I'll ride with Arizona."

Regulus was so cranky and unfriendly. A person would think I had held him at gunpoint to get him here.

He shook his head. "No, you won't. I have a seat to accommodate a second rider and Arizona doesn't." He motioned to the section of seat cushion behind him that sat a little higher. "This is where you sit."

I chewed my thumbnail nervously and looked at Arizona, begging him with my eyes to rescue me from my fate.

"Up you go," Arizona said as he proceeded to move me physically toward the back of Regulus. At least my skirt was long enough to cover the essentials, I thought while grimacing.

"I'm going, I'm going," I muttered in protest. "My dad will kill me for getting onto a motorcycle."

Once I was seated behind Regulus, I adjusted my skirt. He turned and handed me a helmet. Great. I had tried to look better on this outing, and now I was definitely going to have helmet hair.

Before I could argue some more and question where we might be going, Regulus jumped and started his bike. The loud rumbling sound and the vibration of the bike startled me. Arizona hopped on the second bike and started it, nodding at Regulus to lead.

I rested my hands on each side of his body, barely touching him at his belt line on both sides. He grabbed one of my hands to pull it firmly around his waist. I squirmed uncomfortably. Then he captured my left hand and did the same with it. His stomach was solid beneath the shirt. Holy cow, did he do a thousand sit-ups a day?

We rode slowly, crunching gravel and giving me time to adjust to the proximity of his body. He left the driveway and traveled the few feet toward the spot across from my waiting booth.

"Hold on!" He turned his head to yell as he revved the motor with a twist of his hand. I caught my breath and tightened both arms around him, realizing too late that we were going to enter the portal.

As we zipped into the portal, I felt dizzy. The buzzing in my head was immediate but fleeting. My stomach fell like a brick thrown over a cliff in a sensation of free-falling. Just when I thought I could catch my breath, the bottom dropped out in a climatic roller coaster drop. The blackness surrounded us.

***

This must be how death feels. Just a lot of nothing.

Then light blinded me. I squinted my eyes, not prepared for the invasion of white, hot brightness. The buzzing was absent as well as any dizziness. I lifted my face from Regulus's back.

I'd been holding on to him for my life with my body pressed against his and both arms now firmly attached to his waist. I loosened my hold and tried to scoot back on the seat, but the speed of the bike and my recent loss of equilibrium made that difficult.

We zipped along a smooth dirt path at a speed fast enough to scare me. I had never ridden a motorcycle before and tried to concentrate on my surroundings instead of thinking about the precarious ride.

Stone walls rose on both sides of the narrow strip of dirt, and I turned my head to see Arizona riding behind us. I looked up to see how high the buildings reached, maybe three stories. We seemed to be in some sort of alley. Both motorcycles slowed at the end of the alley and turned right and entered a street. There were people lining the road, walking and ignoring us.

Of various heights and sizes, the people walked slowly and a few heads turned to watch us pass by them. They wore shapeless brown robes that seemed to melt into the landscape. We darted around few vehicles and even a man walking with a donkey, loaded with packages. I twisted my head for a second look at the unusual sight.

Hoods concealed individual faces.

And instead of the light bulb of an idea blinking on in my head, the images of the robed figures crackled in my brain like a Fourth of July sparkler. I could see the man in my driveway, his face smashed to my rear car windshield.

The images in my mind must have been combustible because I fought off a burst of fear and anger. I had been excited at the thought of slipping through the portal to some unknown world. But I was in a place where I was likely to be in danger.

"Why did you bring me here?" I yelled into the wind while jabbing Regulus in the side to get his attention. He turned his head, but his helmet prevented me from seeing his face. I tried again, "Tell me what's going on."

We looped around an outdoor market with stands of vegetables in the center and reentered the alley. Arizona still followed close behind. The bike accelerated and, suspecting where Regulus was headed, I lurched forward to hold on tighter. I heard and felt more than saw the blackness ahead. He punched the gas to maneuver us exactly through the portal that now seemed so clear to me. Did it just appear? How did he know exactly where to find it? I made a mental note to ask.

This time, my stomach didn't pitch as much as it had the first time. I had readied myself for the free fall feeling and felt my body, along with Regulus's, glide into nothingness only to slam into the reality of my woods within seconds. We were riding toward my house down the long driveway.

Just to my right, Arizona was grinning, as usual. My dress had hiked up to the tops of my thighs. He couldn't see anything—the dress wasn't that short—but embarrassed, I tried to release one arm from around Regulus to pull my clothing down. The bumpy terrain broke my hold, so I gave up. Arizona's grin widened.

We stopped in a shaded area with a tent, a campfire, and supplies neatly set in a clearing of massive oak, hickory, and pine trees. A fire had been built recently. Cut wood and kindling were tidily stacked on one side.

The campsite wasn't new. My jaw dropped as I absorbed the implications.

"You stay here? You're practically in my backyard, you know. How long did you think you could live out here without anyone finding you?" I shoved off Regulus to swing my leg over and hop from the back of the bike. After the ungraceful dismount, I straightened my full skirt and took off the cardigan, tying its arms around my waist. I had given up on recouping any decorum with my cute outfit.

I peeked inside the tent, just out of plain nosiness, to see if it boasted anything unusual inside. To my disappointment, it looked like the inside of every other camping tent.

I could see Regulus and Arizona out of the corner of my eye taking off helmets and moving the motorcycles.

"We don't live here," Regulus answered me. "It's a temporary camp. We need a place close to the portal. For surveillance."

"Surveillance of my bedroom window?" I said sarcastically picking up a pair of binoculars and squinting to look through the lenses in the direction of my house. "And what was the point of taking me to

Scaryville?"

"It's called Pinaghi, and I wanted you to see how close the world lies to your own. You should understand how easily one can move between these dimensions." Regulus waved his hand at one of the portable chairs.

"Sit."

I wanted to stand just because I didn't like being told to sit, but I realized that it would be silly. I couldn't sit on the ground in the dress. I waited a minute and then sat in a green canvas chair opposite to the one he had offered.

Arizona busied himself stacking wood beside the fire pit. Regulus joined him in the task, and they worked as a team without communicating. Their rhythm told me that they had done this many times before. Arizona squatted beside the pit and piled slivers of bark at the center of the cleared area. A few rocks were stacked at the corners of the perimeter. Regulus carried what appeared to be a storage chest closer to me. An extra chair?

Flames tentatively sparked in the kindling as Arizona blew on the starter. Regulus lifted the lid of the chest that I expected him to sit on. He took out some packages and a pan along with a metal stand that expanded to a grilling surface over the fire. I realized that I was watching dinner preparation.

I was glad for a few minutes to be able to watch Regulus as he opened packages and cooked the meal. He was so strange. He didn't care if I liked him or not. I was having the hardest time figuring out why he was bothering with me. He said that I could find portals, but they had a portal. Why would they need me? I didn't have a good hand of cards in this game.

He, on the other hand, could hold the answers to finding Pete.

"So, yeah, that was pretty awesome and unbelievable, and that's an understatement," I began. "Is that the world that you usually live in?"

"No. But of course, you know that you have had travelers from that world."

"How do you get to your world? A different portal?" I was imagining a portal like a rabbit hole...and hundreds of them throughout my woods.

Regulus handed me a bowl and spoon. He shook his head. "Imagine the portal like a road. You can start out on the same road, but take a turn and end up miles away. The IIA has some control of this portal, and we have programs that allow us to reach certain destinations."

"If the IIA has control, then why don't they just stop people from coming through?" I held my bowl for Arizona as he ladled in a fragrant, thick mixture from the pan. It looked like it might be beef stew. I had been a little hesitant when I saw the packages being opened, but the aroma of the concoction was beyond anything my dad and I ever cooked.

"They have some control, not absolute control."

Regulus picked up a bowl. "And there are some portals in your world that completely escape the control of the

IIA."

"Realllly." I drew out the word, intrigued. "Like where?"

"Many people enter a portal off the coast of Florida. Your people are well aware of it. Yet, individuals are still drawn to it." He ate a tiny bite of stew, then blew on the next spoonful.

"No way. I would have heard of it." I shifted, uncomfortable. What else didn't I know?

"You know of the Bermuda Triangle?" Regulus waited, looking expectant.

"You're kidding, right?" I stared at his serious face and was absolutely sure that he was not.

I waited for him to chew and swallow before my next question. "And people who are sucked into the Bermuda Triangle... Where do they go?"

He shrugged. "It's unknown. I told you that the IIA doesn't control the travels throughout that portal. There are an endless number of dimensions that the aimless traveler can fall into. That's why it is extremely important that the IIA program the course of the traveler. Otherwise, your destination can be unfortunate as well as producing unnatural consequences."

"You sound like a commercial for the IIA," I stated between bites. "Doesn't man have free will to seek his own destiny?" For a minute, I felt that my speech pattern had actually mimicked Regulus's in its formality.

"We protect the universes," Arizona said defensively. "Your world is so bent on planetary suicide, it's a miracle it's still around."

I looked at Arizona. Usually he seemed like he was on my side. "Your world, you said. This is our world, Arizona. You said you were born in Phoenix, that is, if you were telling me the truth." My mind fleetingly went to the connection between Arizona's name and his birthplace. "It's our world. I don't know where you're from, Regulus, but our world does just fine."

"I am from the IIA." Regulus sounded pompous and self-important as he tossed his bowl into a plastic tub.

"Why do you even care about this world if the IIA is so great?" I couldn't figure out why I had gotten so defensive about it.

"Because your world is our seed vault," Regulus said.

All I could picture at the mention of a seed vault was my grandmother's kitchen drawer that held her beloved Burpee seed packets. Seeds for beefsteak tomatoes and all kinds of flowers. I last visited my grandparents in Clearwater, Florida when I was fifteen. A month of Florida could have been heaven. But it hadn't been. After Pete disappeared, my dad had taken time off from work to hit the road looking for him. And I'd been stuck in Clearwater.

I'd heard him on the phone one night with my

grandfather. "Dad, I think he might have gone to find Nancy. If that's where he went, I'll bring him back." Dad never talked about her. The woman who was once my mother.

"Mia, this is part of your training. Are you even paying attention?"

"No, I'm eating." I clanged my spoon against the bowl with unnecessary force. Looking down, I realized that I had eaten half of the meal, a thick stew of beef, peas, carrots, onion with just the right seasonings. How that delectable meal came out of a bag, I couldn't even begin to comprehend. Much better than my usual sandwich at home.

"Regulus, you need to break it down," I said. "Tell me what you mean when you say seed vault. It's like you talk in code all the time."

Regulus sat on the chest beside me and kicked his feet out in front of him. Darkness had fallen while we'd eaten and talked. A cicada chirp vibrated through the clearing. Stars had begun to glitter against the backdrop of the sky. Arizona looked up to follow my gaze.

"A seed vault is a preservation of life. You keep the starter seeds safely locked away and ready for use in case of loss of life and the need for a new beginning," Regulus said. "Your people have a seed vault for the so-called doomsday. It's in the Arctic. It is a storage facility holding a genetic diversity of seeds for food crops."

"And you guys are keeping your seeds here?" "No, our seeds are different," Regulus answered.

"Your people are our seeds."

"Like an ark, but instead of two of each, there's

DNA to represent millions of possibilities," Arizona said.

"So, Earth is like the ark." I frowned, stating this more to myself than in response to the conversation.

"The IIA works to protect you from outsiders. It's your destiny to protect the Earth from destruction," Regulus said. "As well as from disease, genetic mutation, and dimensional tampering."

I thought about global warming, pollution, and all the other environmental topics that were discussed in my science class last year. It just didn't make sense to pick Earth.

"So, what is it that you think I can do in all this? And don't you think saying it's my destiny is a little over the top?" It's your destiny... I could hear wise ObiWan's voice in my head. I had watched the old Star Wars movies with Dad a million times.

Arizona scooted his chair closer to mine as if to tell me a secret. "We have been informed that there is someone harboring the Slips as they come through the portal. The last Slip bargained for mercy with the IIA. The Slip confessed that he was to meet someone here for safe harbor. Help us find this individual who will destroy your world."

Great. I had enough problems without the weight of the world added. "I can try, but I don't see how I can figure out who it is," I said to Arizona. Find some other Jedi, I thought.

"It is a male individual at Whispering Woods College," Regulus said.

"OK, you didn't say that you had it narrowed down to a few thousand people," I said, failing to hold the sarcasm level down.

"The Slip had a meeting time and location. The individual from the university will be expecting to meet a young female Slip. We want you to go to this place. Arizona and I will be there out of sight and ready to retrieve the criminal," Regulus said.

"We would never let anything happen to you." Arizona settled his hand on my knee, and I didn't take it as a lewd gesture, but rather a comforting one. I was getting used to the fact that Arizona was the touchy-feely type.

I covered Arizona's hand with mine, and then lifted it to take it off my knee. He grinned.

"And if I do this...if I am the bait...you can then help me with information about finding Pete," I said in my best no-nonsense tone.

"We have already agreed to that, Mia," said Arizona.

Regulus handed me a piece of paper. "Here is the information for the meeting. You will travel alone to the location at the set time. You must wear this attached to your clothing."

The gold pin was the size of a half-dollar and looked like a tree branch. Oh goody. I'd be dressed in Grandma's hand-me-down jewelry. I held it up to the area above my heart and raised my eyebrows while nodding that I got it.

I examined the note. "OK, I think I can find this.

And this says 18:30. That's military time stuff, right?

It doesn't tell me the date." "Tomorrow night," answered Regulus.

"Why didn't the Slip go to meet the person right after coming here? Why the gap in time? And what about the baby? How was that guy going to take care of a baby in the woods until tomorrow night? And where's that baby's mother?" The rush of questions poured from my lips.

"You ask too many questions, Mia. The strategy of a Slip is not your concern. As for the baby, not all babies have natural mothers. Some have Makers and, later, Caretakers," Regulus said in his authoritative manner.

For some unknown reason that statement made me sad. Not for myself but for him.

My noisy ring tone startled me, and I jumped. I took my cell phone from my pocket to show Regulus and Arizona, who had also reacted to music seemingly pouring out of nowhere.

I saw the name on the caller ID. "Hey, Em, what's up?"

"Are you back from the date yet?" she said breathlessly.

"I told you, it's not like that," I said, trying not to reveal too much to Regulus and Arizona. I turned my back to them. "And no, I am not home yet, but I'll call you when I get there."

"Don't forget...sorry to call. Do you know what time it is? I've been going crazy wanting to hear, and I couldn't imagine that you wouldn't be home yet."

I cut into her chatter. "Bye, Em, I'll call."

"Eek, sorry...'bye."

"Was your call of great importance?" Regulus asked.

"No, nothing, Em just wanted to talk," I said. They both stared at me, waiting.

"You know, just girl talk." They both just looked at

me, clearly puzzled.

"It's teenage girl bonding stuff," I said. "What's up, whatcha doin'...you know."

Regulus looked at Arizona for an explanation and only got a shrug.

I looked at the paper in my hand again. "OK..." I cleared my throat. "I really need to go home now. You know, I do have school and all."

Regulus and Arizona stood to put out the fire, and I sat and watched since I didn't know what I should do. I examined the tent again and looked at the rolled-up sleeping bags. I had never been camping except for in a two-man tent in the backyard with my brother as a child. We didn't have to go far to explore the wilderness.

"How long have you guys been camping here so close to my house?" I asked, wondering how they had avoided discovery.

"A couple of weeks." Regulus returned some supplies to the storage chest he had been sitting on earlier, moving with mesmerizing grace and speed. He was built like a football player. A lean one without an ounce of fat on him. He looked up and met my eyes. My cheeks were instantly on fire. Look away, I told myself, but was unable to follow my own directions from my brain.

"Where do you guys stay? I mean, where do you live?" I blurted out, looking at the tent and breaking the eye contact.

"Wherever the IIA stations us," Regulus said. "We are registered at the university. This campsite is necessary as a second station away from the dorm."

Arizona grimaced as he added, "I like a place with

a
hot shower and a Taco Bell, to be honest. Your portal location demanded less than desirable living conditions until we moved into the dorm."

Regulus went to his motorcycle and beckoned me by waving his hand and motioning for me to take my seat behind him. I didn't argue but gathered my skirt high enough to allow my leg to swing over. I gripped his shoulder to steady myself as I threw my leg over the seat and before I could protest, he grabbed my waist to help me. I looked over his shoulder to avoid his eyes.

He started the engine, accelerating within seconds, heading through the trees and brush on a route that would take us to my driveway. My log house appeared before me in minutes and the trip had been too short for me to think of any questions about what would take place tomorrow.

I could hear Biscuit barking and spotted my dog in the front window. I got off the bike before Regulus could help and straightened my clothes. I took off the helmet that I had used and handed it to him.

"Thanks for the dinner. I'll do my part tomorrow night. Just don't get me killed or anything." I laughed nervously.

"Loyalty and teamwork is part of our training. If you don't make it out alive, we all don't," said Arizona.

"Don't you think you're being a little melodramatic?" I ran my fingers through my hair, imagining the helmet hairdo.

"This is our bonding. You prove to us that you are part of this team, and we are loyal to you," Regulus said.

I walked away before I could argue that I didn't want to be part of their team. Biscuit, my dad, Pete, Austin, and Em were my homies. Strangers from another dimension, no matter how good-looking, were not. I chanted this to myself as I walked up the steps of my porch with the memory of Regulus's intense blue eyes burning in my brain.

***

I logged onto Quest for Zion, tucking my feet underneath my bottom in the swivel desk chair. My soft cotton pajamas felt much better than the uncomfortable dress I had stupidly worn earlier. I broke off bite-size pieces of strawberry Pop-Tart to nibble on. My dad had written me an e-mail earlier in the day, and I clicked back and forth between his e-mail and the Quest screen.

Why had Dad changed his mind about GameCon? That was so like a parent.

Now when I didn't want to go, Dad said he might change his mind about letting me. Austin would probably say that registration had closed anyway. Gamers from all over the country would be attending, and there would not be a hotel room in a twenty mile radius of the convention center.

My dad wasn't usually wishy-washy, but he must have felt guilty for giving me so much responsibility and treating me like an adult on the one hand but refusing to let me go out of town with Em and Austin.

I toggled back to the screen and could see Austin and Em were both online. Em was peeved because I wouldn't give her any information other than saying that we had eaten in town, which of course was a lie. Austin hadn't mentioned the dinner. He wasn't even chatting with me online. I knew that he didn't want to hear any of the details.

So, my two best friends in the whole world were giving me the silent treatment, even after my tentative "hi" in the chat box to both. An animated pigeon went flying across the screen with a scrolled letter attached to its foot and landed on a stone wall image in the top right of my screen. I clicked on it and broke off another piece of pastry.

"Don't trust them. Meet me at the ocean at suppertime."

I froze as I read the message. I looked at the line above the message to see the sender, and my stomach clenched into a hard knot. I dropped the piece of PopTart poised at my mouth. The sender line said the message was from closetmonsterslayer@hotmail.com. There was only one person in the universe that I knew as the Closet Monster Slayer.

My palms were sweaty as I hurriedly typed a reply message, "What ocean? When?" I hit the send button within seconds.

I held my breath waiting for a reply. A second later it came: "Invalid user address."

"What do you mean, invalid address!" I screamed at the monitor. I opened up the message again from Closet Monster Slayer. I typed the message slowly and hit the send button again. Take a deep breath, I told myself. The server just hit a glitch. Of course, the address had to be valid. You can't receive an e-mail from an invalid one.

I stared at the computer screen, the words glaring at me. Another message saying "Invalid user address." I sat back in my swivel desk chair and covered my eyes with my hands. Was Pete out there online sending me a message on *Quest of Zion*? And what did it mean? Who was I not supposed to trust?

Actually that wasn't a hard one to figure out. It had to be referencing the IIA—Regulus and Arizona. But telling me to meet him at the ocean... That was crazy. Like I would know which ocean and place. I would do it, of course, if I knew where and when. My dad would obviously ground me for life, but it would be worth it.

I looked at my monitor, hoping for a new message before letting my head fall to the desk on my hands. I swallowed hard to stop myself from crying. I thought of Pete and how glad I was just to know that he was alive.

And then I remembered him shouting at the video game he was playing. "C'mon man, just meet me at the ocean," he would yell at the other computer-generated player. I would fall into giggles at his frustration and join him, saying, "Yeah, you dodo, just meet him at the ocean."

I jerked my head up in glee. He didn't mean that I should meet him at the real ocean. He was talking about a video game. And I knew just where I would have a chance to meet him.

I picked up my cell phone and hit the quick dial key for Austin.

"Hi, Mia, what's up?"

"I can go to GameCon after all. Do you think it's

too late to get a couple of rooms at the convention hotel? And I know we'll have to pay late registration and all—" I squirmed in my chair and hoped that my voice didn't give me away. I'd have to lie to my dad and to Austin to pull this one off. "No problemo, my friend." He sounded excited.

"Really? I mean, I still have to see if Em's parents will let her go. And that's if she is speaking to me. She got mad at me for not sharing enough info with her."

"I said, no problem. I reserved the two rooms back when we first talked about going. I haven't cancelled yet since I have a twenty-four hour window for doing it."

"You're the best, Austin," I said, and I meant it.

"I know, babe. Just make up with Em and be ready for a blast of a weekend."

"Cool, I will."

I hung up and immediately called Em. Making up with her was easier that I thought it might be, since we so rarely argued about anything. After she went to beg her parents to let her go, I wrote my dad an e-mail to tell him that I wanted to spend the weekend at Em's house, and then I wrote some extra lines telling him about my classes and my science project. I found it hard to concentrate since my mind was skipping from the excitement of the message from Pete and the problem of being mixed up with Regulus and Arizona.

I had already said that I would help them with the capture of the person harboring Slips. What would they do to me if I backed out?

Chapter Ten

Regulus

Regulus watched Mia walking along the worn brick sidewalk boldly ignoring the dark shadows and hidden alcoves of the older building. Arizona stood beside him as still as one of the columns flanking the sidewalk. They had both hidden in the shadows, dark, militant clothing blending into the landscape of oak trees and artfully planted hedges. His stomach knotted in trepidation as he watched the young girl, almost woman, study the dull metal door plates in search of the correct numbers. She never faltered in her stride that took her forward, only slowing down at each door. Her tennis shoes made no sound, and she was graceful in her purposeful hunt. Regulus knew that she had no idea of the true danger that could present itself tonight in this place.

Arizona leaned back against a tree, relaxed while watching the girl.

"She's going to the door. Why is she moving so fast?" Regulus muttered.

"Because she is a woman on a mission," Arizona answered in a singsong voice and smiled.

"She doesn't have a clue. She thinks that this will all be over soon," Regulus said through gritted teeth. "She's too trusting. How does she know that we will protect her and not cause her harm?"

"She's loyal to her friends," Arizona said smugly. "She is especially fond of me," he added with a twinkle in his eye.

Regulus desperately wanted to slam his knuckles into Arizona's white teeth. Instead he turned back to realize that Mia had disappeared in that second of distraction. Muttering an oath and tapping Arizona hard on the chest, he pointed to the building. The shadows had deepened as the sun was setting, and Regulus shoved off from the trunk of the tree that had shielded him from view. Since he hadn't seen Mia actually enter, he scanned the area to be certain that she had stepped through the door instead of hesitating at the side.

Regulus strode over to stand at the right of the doorway. Prior observation told him that the campus would be virtually deserted at this time of day. Arizona withdrew to stand ten feet away, pretending to read a bulletin he picked up from the ground. Regulus stuck his hand in his pocket, palming the small weapon while he blanked his mind of thoughts of Mia. His target was near, and he had better get his priorities in order.

He took the doorknob, preparing to enter when the heavy wood door opened inward. He slid away a few feet and held his weapon against his leg. Mia exited first, and he braced himself. She was transparent in the way she shook her head in a "no" gesture without making eye contact to indicate that she didn't want him to approach them. Instinct said to move toward her and take her out of the throng of people who had walked out of the building. He held back.

Something was off. Why would the Slip give an incorrect meeting place or time? This group leaving the assigned rendezvous was all wrong. He watched as Mia stood to the side and waited. He urged her with his eyes to continue. She ignored him. She approached a large man wearing small glasses and holding a bulging leather briefcase. Regulus watched her face become animated as she talked with him, gesturing and smiling. The man returned her smile and nodded toward a building opposite of the one they had left.

Mia walked with the man, and Regulus looked at Arizona quizzically. The cell phone in his pocket vibrated. He took it out to see a text from Mia, who had apparently kept his number. When had she texted him? Then he noticed her hand shoved into her jean pocket, and he marveled at her talent of texting by touch alone.

The message read, "Know him. It's OK."

Regulus nodded toward them and followed at a distance as they entered a building with a large sign reading "Whispering Woods U Eatery." The big cafeteria was filled with students perusing stations with different types of food. This explained the lack of students outside during this time of day. His nerves were strained to capacity as he tried to follow

Mia and the big man. They wove in and out of the crowd of students talking at tables and selecting food.

They stopped in front of a coffee counter to order and the man pulled bills of out of his wallet to pay. The pair carried their drinks to an empty table.

Regulus felt someone staring at him. Arizona, beside him, waited for the next move. He looked up to see the boy, Austin, walking toward them.

Arizona stuck out his hand in greeting. "Hey man, nice to see ya."

"What's up, guys? I haven't seen you around the campus since I met you at Mia's," Austin said in a suspicious tone as he slowly shook Arizona's hand.

"Yeah, this is our first time in here," Arizona said with displeasure. "Thought we might need to live on more than fast food and macaroni and cheese. We're both freshmen."

Austin was listening to Arizona but looking at Regulus.

"Hello there, Austin." Regulus tried to sound friendly, but he could tell it came out stilted. He didn't care for this one, and he could tell the hostility was mutual.

"I saw you looking at Mia over there," Austin said. "Does she know you're here?"

"Ah, no," he answered. "I just noticed her. We don't want to interrupt her. She seems to be engaged in an important conversation."

"Nah, that's just her mentor for her science project," Austin said. "You know she's too young to go here. She's just a senior in high school."

"Yes, I knew that," Regulus said to him

deliberately. He stepped a little closer into Austin's personal space.

Austin took a step back. "Sure you did," he stated coolly. "Just thought you might want to know you're messing with jail bait. And she's my girl."

Regulus gave his rival a narrow and knowledgeable smile. "If she's yours, you have nothing to worry about." He wondered if Mia's visit with the man would end soon. He was ready to be away from this place with so many people.

Mia stood, and he sensed she was saying good-bye.

"We have an appointment, Arizona. We should be going," Regulus said.

"Places to go, people to see," Arizona answered while looking at Austin. "Hopefully, we'll meet again soon."

As Regulus walked through the tables, he looked at the young people talking animatedly about unimportant topics. He heard laughter, sensed that the conversations were lighthearted and free. He tried to imagine a life such as theirs. He passed a table with a couple kissing and caressing each other in this public place. He bumped their table abruptly and startled them as he went by it.

Arizona chortled.

Chapter Eleven

Plea for Help

Dr. Bleeker held the cup to his mouth and sipped coffee. I stared at him, not knowing what to say. He put down the cup and took out a shiny black cell phone, holding the small screen so the display would face me.

"See this little boy. This is my youngest, Michael." The blond kid looked happy sitting on the carousel horse. "He watched his mother being taken from our home. They took her in the middle of the night."

I could feel Dr. Bleeker's eyes searching my tiniest reaction. He pressed a button on his screen and held up another picture. "Ethan, he's thirteen now."

"They, who?" I answered, still refusing to concede that he might be part of this drama. I concentrated on removing the plastic lid of my coffee cup and blew over the top. The chattering around us almost drowned out my response.

"The IIA, Mia. Why are you part of this?" Dr.
Bleeker furrowed his brow in disappointment.
"Why are you helping them?"

"Because I don't know what else to do. I'm freaked
out. I thought I was handling it."

"You're handling yourself fine." His voice soothed
me. "You also have a family to protect, right? A
father, grandparents..."

I felt a chill at the mention of my dad. "Leave my
dad out of this. This is something I am supposed to
be dealing with, not him, or anyone else."

"Careful, or your friends will know that something
is not right." The words edged in on me in a dark
green menacing swirl, at odds with the laugh lines
around his eyes. He smiled sympathetically, and the
creases deepened.

I nodded and I tried to give him a smile. I hoped it
didn't look as fake as it felt.

"I'm trying to protect your father as I would have
protected my wife...if I could have."

"Why did they take her? I mean, they had to have
a reason."

"She had a genetic disease," he said softly as he
examined his paper cup. I saw an unmistakable
sadness in his face. "Their intolerance is
unimaginable. I am at your mercy. My children are
at your mercy." I remained quiet.

He continued, "I am begging you to reconsider
what you're doing."

"And what is it, Dr. Bleeker? I really don't know
what I'm doing. I was just supposed to meet someone
here today. I think I was supposed to be the bait," I
said while watching him take another drink of the

scalding hot liquid. "What can I do?"

"Give me until Monday to leave with my children. Pretend that you don't know why I left. Don't give me away to them. Don't pronounce a death sentence on Michael and Ethan."

"I'll think about it. I mean I don't want anything to happen to your kids. Why can't you leave now? Pack and leave." I attempted to keep my face unreadable.

"There are some loose ends that I must tie up. There are others depending on me. Just give me a few days. I'll take my family and leave by Monday."

I saw Regulus and Arizona out of the corner of my eye talking with Austin. They were walking toward the exit.

I rose to leave. "I'll do my best to stall them.

They're not stupid. What will I tell them about talking to you?"

"You'll tell them the truth. I'm your mentor. We are working together on your senior project." Dr. Bleeker's voice was calm and matter-of-fact.

I nodded as I stood and turned to walk toward the doors leading outside. Austin was already coming toward me, weaving quickly in and out between tables.

"Hi," Austin said as he came to an abrupt stop inches away from me, nodding to acknowledge us. "Dr.

Bleeker..."

Dr. Bleeker returned the nod with a carefree smile as I said to Austin, "I was just leaving." I met Dr. Bleeker's eyes and murmured, "Good-bye, Dr. Bleeker."

Austin accompanied me, draping his left arm

casually over my shoulders. The physical movement was a tentative one and he withdrew his arm when he looked into my eyes.

"What's wrong, Mia?"

"I can't talk about it, Austin. Can you just be my friend right now?"

"Sure," he answered seriously. "Whatever it is, you know I'm here for you. Dr. Bleeker say something about your project to upset you?"

I wanted to cry at the sincerity in his voice. Good ol' Austin had always been there for me.

He grabbed my hand and held it. "Let's get outta here. We can go ride four-wheelers or hang at your house or mine."

I didn't say anything. I had decisions to make and couldn't think about going to do the fun stuff that normal teenagers do.

Austin must have misread my hesitation and said, "Unless you have plans with Tweedledee and Tweedledum... I saw they were hanging out in here. Strange dudes." I didn't respond. "I mean, do they always show up together? They got a real bromance going on—"

"Stop it, Austin. I know you don't like them, but I don't want to talk about them right now."

We walked through the doors, and I half expected to see Regulus and Arizona waiting to cuff me or something equally dramatic. Did they know that I was talking with the enemy? Did they even have a clue? My throat constricted in panic at the thought of my dad being in any danger. I walked with Austin to the parking lot nearest the cafeteria and unlocked my car while he waited.

He leaned against the car door. That stopped me from getting into my car and fleeing. He took my forearms and pulled me close to his chest. "I don't know what Regulus did to you, but I'll make sure that he stays away from you." He rubbed my back.

I pulled away. His assumption that Regulus had done something to me surprised me. I had been sitting with Dr. Bleeker. "Why do you think he's the one who's upset me?"

"Because I saw him watching you. He looks at you like he owns you. He's bad news."

I glanced around to see if we were alone. Of course, we were not. There were students walking around the campus now that the dinner hour had passed. Someone called out hello to Austin and he waved back.

I smiled at Austin. "Why don't you come over and hang out? It will be too dark to ride four-wheelers when we get home, but I could use an hour or so of Quest."

"Sure thing. I'll follow you there," he said without a bit of hesitation.

I felt a little guilty because I could tell he might be reading more into my invitation than I had intended. "I need a good friend tonight, Austin. I want it to be like old times."

"Of course. Isn't it always?" he asked as if I had requested something silly. He mussed my hair as my brother might have and turned to head toward his Jeep, parked in the middle of the lot.

Austin jumped into the driver's seat and guided his vehicle to wait in the parking row for me to lead. I put the key into the ignition and nearly shot out of my seat at a rapping on my window.

Dr. Bleeker stood there, moving his finger in a circular motion to signal that I should roll down the glass. I started the car and pushed the electric window button, unwilling to exit the car.

"Since we've just visited, we can forget about the meeting tomorrow afternoon," he said. "It would look odd for you to be on campus two days in a row. Looks like you'll be needing a new mentor anyway. Right?"

Actually, I had already forgotten about it in light of the more pressing issues of trying to play secret agent girl. "Uh, OK, whatever you say, Dr. Bleeker," I awkwardly mumbled. I looked in my mirror and could see Austin patiently waiting. He lifted his hands up in a questioning gesture.

Dr. Bleeker patted the car door in the same manner that you might send a horse off in the Wild West, and I backed up to start my trip home.

***

The lights were on in the house as I approached, and my dad sat on the front porch swing. I couldn't get out of my car fast enough. Austin parked a little ways off the driveway and joined me.

"Dad, what are you doing back?" I said breathlessly as I looked to the right and left for any evidence of Regulus and Arizona.

"Came back early. I was worried when I got home and wondered where you might be. Is your cell phone on?"

I looked at my phone, which had been in silent ringer mode. "Nope, I was at the university. Oh, wow, sorry about that."

"It's OK. Hi there, Austin. You looking out for my girl while I'm gone?"

"You know it." Austin looked a little antsy.

"Thanks, Austin, for seeing Mia home. It's nice to know that I can trust you with her." My dad turned to me. "Mia, I came home early because I have to go out of town again this weekend. I've felt somewhat guilty that I said you couldn't go to the Gaming Wars conference with Emily and Austin. Is it too late for me to change my mind?"

"GameCon, Dad, not Gaming Wars." I looked nervously at Austin. He already thought I had been given the go-ahead.

He was surprised, but he wasn't going to give me away. "I got it covered, Mr. Taylor, no problem."

"Thanks." Dad guided me inside the house with a hand on my shoulder. "See you later, Austin. Call Mia if you can still go."

As we walked up the steps of the porch, I marveled at the turn of events. Maybe I could avoid Regulus and Arizona while my dad was home and then I could leave for GameCon. I was sure that this would buy me some time to think about what I should do. In the meantime, I was anxious to log into Quest and see if I had any new messages. If that message had been from Pete, and I was sure that it was, I was about to get my brother back.

Nothing else mattered.

No new messages were in the Quest system when I logged in, and I began to fear that I had dreamed the entire thing. I had checked it late so I could visit with my dad and wrongly assumed that I would fall into an exhausted sleep upon my head meeting the pillow. I spent the night switching sleeping positions from left side to right, to my back, and over again.

School was a test of my willpower as I walked from class to class in a zombie state. Em was excited to be going to GameCon, even though her mother was chaperoning us. The original plan had been to ride with Austin to Dallas. There would be two hotel rooms, one for me and Em and the other for Austin and maybe one of his friends.

That plan was now extinct. Em's parents had declared that hell would freeze over before she would be going unchaperoned to Dallas. So, Em's mom, Peggy Sue, came up with what she declared a brilliant plan. Peggy Sue would go with us and do some shopping while the "teenagers" went to GameCon. Em vacillated between being thrilled to get to GameCon and pouting over the fact that her mom was tagging along. I had convinced Em that I should ride with Austin so he wouldn't be bored.

After school, I drove home past the waiting booth holding my breath. My paranoia had reached an all-time high as I wondered who and what might be waiting for me along the way. The creepiness factor had also risen. Regulus and Arizona popping into my life with information about alternate dimensions was mind-blowing enough, but the fact that Dr. Bleeker and my brother knew about the IIA had me thinking I might need psych counseling.

The night was fairly uneventful as Friday nights go.

Em sent me half a dozen texts asking what I was going to wear, while I responded that I didn't know and didn't care. I could tell that she wasn't pleased with my responses, so I ended up texting the contents of my suitcase as I haphazardly threw T-shirts and jeans into it. I spent the rest of the night compulsively checking the Quest message box to see if I had any new messages.

We planned to leave early the next morning, which suited me just fine. My dad left for the airport as I waited for Austin to pick me up. I checked the window every two seconds in anticipation. Once, I thought I saw movement in the woods. I was sure that I was being watched.

Austin didn't even need to knock on the door as I was out on the porch before he could.

"I'm ready, let's go."

He glanced at me with a surprised look. I sprinted to his Jeep and threw my duffle bag into the back seat.

"Hold your horses, little lady," Austin said with a drawl. "You know that Mrs. Peggy Sue and Em will keep us waiting if we get to their house too early."

"Yes, that's why I told them that we'd be there thirty minutes ago. Now, they'll be ready on time."

"Girl, you are too smart!"

Austin looked as happy as I had ever seen him. He was whistling a tune and turned up the radio. He bobbed his head to the beat as we departed my driveway and entered the highway. Basically, he was in his own little world, which explained why he didn't see the figure standing in the shadows of the oak trees near my waiting booth.

I tried to ignore what I saw and to close my ears to the humming that came from the portal entrance.

Em's mom drove a Suburban, and we tried to keep up while she broke every speed limit. We had traveled a hundred miles before Austin finally asked what I had dreaded. "How is it that your dad gave you the go-ahead after you told me that you could go?"

I was glad that he had fastened the top on the Jeep so we would be able to talk because I had been waiting for this moment. "I was going whether he said I could or not."

"That doesn't sound like you. What's up with you?"

"I got a message the other day on Quest."

"And?"

"I think the message was from Pete."

"Somebody's just messing with you. Why would he send you a note and not just call or text?"

"I don't know. The note was like an encrypted message that no one would understand but me."

"Why would he do that? He wouldn't be in that much trouble if he just came home."

"That's what scares me. So, here's where I am gonna ask you to do something for me. It's major important that I know I can count on you."

Austin looked over at me somberly. "Anything. Pete was my friend, too."

"Is your friend. He's out there, and I think he's going to meet me at GameCon."

"Tell me what I need to do."

"Make sure that I'm not seen meeting him. Help me get to a certain game booth without being followed."

"Who's following you? Is the stalker dude,

Regulus?"

"It might be anyone. I'm not really sure." I managed a smile.

Austin looked confused, but didn't press me for more answers. He opened his cell, and I guessed it must have been vibrating.

"Sure, Mrs. Peggy Sue." He looked at me while rolling his eyes.

"Gonna have to pull over for a bathroom," he said as he plunked down his cell phone. "Does that make three stops so far?"

"Four, if you count the one before we left town."

He shook his head in disgust. "Four."

***

As soon as we got to Dallas, we checked into the hotel. The front desk check-in was somewhat embarrassing, because Em's mom kept going on and on about how great the hotel was and how thankful she was that Austin hadn't booked us at a roach motel. We stored the suitcases in the rooms and promised to keep our phones on if Mrs. Peggy Sue needed to check on us.

In the elevator, I nervously looked at Austin, who winked at me. We approached the registration table in the Grand Hall of the hotel to pick up our bags and badges. A young man sat marking an attendee roster. He looked up our names and enthusiastically began to tell us the layout of the conference rooms and vendor booths.

I checked my watch. The message had referred to suppertime. At my house that had always been 5:00

p.m. If Pete were going to be at the booth, he'd arrive at that time. I had a few hours, so I followed Austin and Em through the throngs of people. We left the vendor area to attend a demo on setting up a guild in a new RPG game. After the session, we had to stop by the restrooms for Em and I waited with Austin in the hallway.

"When are you going to need the distraction?" Austin asked.

"What?"

"You know, when you said you need help in getting to a booth without being followed."

"Oh, at five. What are you going do?" I quickly asked, wanting to know before Em came out.

Austin held the phone up to his ear. "Tiny, it's me, man. Five o'clock. Thanks."

"Tiny?"

"I made a phone call while you guys went into that last quick stop. Called Tiny. He's somewhat of a...gaming maven. You can count on me, remember?"

I nodded as Em came to join us in the hallway. She looked from Austin to me and asked, "Why the serious faces? Let's go have some fun."

We looked at the schedule and headed off for another meeting room. I studied the people walking though the wide hallways. There were mostly guys, but more females than I might have guessed. People were standing in lines leading into some of the sessions that were more popular, like the discussion panels and interactive demos. I found myself scanning for a familiar face. I was sure that Regulus had been watching me from the edge of the woods earlier today.

At 4:40 p.m., I feared that I might die of stress-related anxiety. I was simultaneously excited to see Pete but afraid to see him lest I was followed. I put in my ear buds and turned on my iPod. I concentrated on listening to the music instead of thinking.

It was almost time. Austin nudged me since I hadn't heard him. "Let's go check out the exhibit hall."

I took out my ear buds and nodded.

We walked into the door and continued to skim the outside perimeter in a clockwise loop, stopping at the third booth to look at gaming T-shirts.

I examined my wrist. One minute.

"I'm going to the restroom. I'll be back in a second," I said to Austin and Em. Em made a movement as though she wanted to accompany me, so I held up my hand. "Be right back." I hurried off.

I knew exactly where the booth was located since I had studied my exhibit map for hours. I tried to walk briskly without taking off in a full-fledged run. The exhibit hall attendance had tripled since earlier in the day. The sessions must have been boring at this time. I was amazed to see how thick the crowd had gotten.

I walked through the middle aisle and wished I were taller so I could see past the people in front of me. I had approximately five more booths to go before I would reach the one I'd been thinking about all day.

The Atlantis booth.

A tall guy knocked into me as though he wasn't

paying attention. He didn't even say, "Excuse me, sorry." I frowned at him, but he was looking at the aisle behind me with a big confused grin on his face. I took a second to follow his gaze.

Everywhere I looked, there were suddenly teenagers and adults holding cardboard swords. Not exactly swords... to be specific they were light sabers. Not everyone held one, but there was a throng in the middle aisle jousting with them. Others had stopped to watch the outbreak of swordplay and try to figure out what was going on. Even the vendors had stopped their sales pitches and networking to watch in amazement.

Simultaneously, the theme to Star Wars had roared from the loudspeakers and the jousting was in time with the music. I had to break my attention from the scene playing out and run for the Atlantis booth. I wedged my way between two guys dueling with their make-believe weapons. The end of the aisle was not as crowded as the middle, and I shoved a gawker aside to reach my destination.

The sales reps for *Atlantis: Home at Last* were as enthralled by the flash mob as the conference attendees. They were standing in front of their booth, shaking their heads and laughing at the pandemonium.

I looked around for any sign of my brother. The booth was empty. With the sales reps standing in the exhibit hall aisle, the booth was deserted. I turned from left to right, looking for Pete. I couldn't stop the overwhelming stab in my chest at the emptiness I saw before me. I stared at the table, neatly covered with a white tablecloth and several promo items. The vendors had obviously gotten smart and displayed only a few so attendees could take just one.

That's when I saw it. A typical onlooker would never have noticed it. The vendors would have thrown it away.

A business card lay on the table with a penny on top like a paperweight. I grabbed them and shoved both in my pocket.

I slunk through the crowd. The music stopped, and the flash mob participants stopped their swordplay. I was too deep in my own thoughts to hear Emily until she poked me in the ribs.

"Ow, that hurt."

"Where did you go? You missed the whole thing."

"What thing?"

"See, I told you. She missed it," Em told Austin.

"Nah, she didn't, did ya?"

"Oh, yeah, that was crazy. Why were people doing that?" I asked, trying to seem interested.

"A friend of mine told me that GameCon would love to help out with a flash mob if someone set it up," Austin said with a wink. "That was rad. Much better than the kind where people freeze in place."

"Yeah, cool," I muttered.

"I'm starving," Em said. "Let's find some food."

"Your wish is my command." Austin led the way to the massive double doors.

As we followed Austin, I glanced over my shoulder in time to make eye contact with a middle-aged man sporting a crew cut. He seemed to be walking quickly to catch up with someone. I looked back again, sure that the stalker was a figment of my imagination.

Mr. Crew Cut made eye contact, and he smiled

with dark gray menace. His face didn't read the friendly, "Hi kid, we're all having a good time, now aren't we?" type of smile. His response was a creepy, acknowledging smile and showed just enough teeth to look dangerous. And he finished off the smile with a salute as he picked up the pace toward me.

Chapter Twelve

Friendships

I walked at a rapid pace, looking over my shoulder as nonchalantly as possible, if there is such a thing. It's pretty evident that you think someone is after you when you spend every third step twisting your head to the left or right for a better view.

"Slow down, I'm not that hungry." Em laughed.

The long corridor went on forever. I dizzied at the patterns in the red and gold carpet. My heart was racing, and I had to fight panic when I looked ahead to see Mr. Crew Cut coming toward me. That was just not possible. He had been behind me. I looked back and saw the original one still behind us.

Great, there were two of them. Were they part of the IIA? I heard Dr. Bleeker's voice in my head: *They took her in the middle of the night.* I had pictured Regulus and Arizona when he had said that. Who were these guys?

My options were limited. My first option was to turn and run. I was a decent runner. But I was counting on being able to outrun them. And then what?

I took my second option.

I pivoted toward the red box mounted on the wall and jammed my fingers into the area labeled "pull down." The lever handle went down with one yank.

The fire alarm pulsated in a high-pitched warning buzz. I caught a glimpse of Em's shocked expression. Doors along the corridor immediately swung open and attendees poured out of each room. A lady wearing a navy hotel uniform ushered people in the direction of the exits.

The hallway filled with people in seconds, and I lost sight of Mr. Crew Cut One and Two. All I could see were bodies in front and back of me. I grabbed Em's and Austin's hands, hauling them through the crowd.

Everyone went outside. The noise level made it difficult to talk so I nodded my head in a direction away from the hotel. I took off the GameCon nametag and discreetly tucked it into my pocket. Em and Austin followed my lead in going incognito. An amazing number of people had flooded out due to the fire alarm. We easily got lost in the sea of bodies that flowed to the street corner, blending into other pedestrians in the crosswalk. I had chanced a look at Em to see that she was confused and horrified over me pulling the fire alarm, but Austin didn't seem fazed in the least. Did he usually hang out with people who pulled those kinds of crazy stunts? It hadn't registered in my mind yet that I had just done something that extreme. Could I go to jail if someone had seen me? I guess jail would be better than disappearing with the IIA.

We were several blocks from the hotel when Em finally found her voice. "For crying out loud, are you out of your freaking mind?"

"Do you think anybody saw me pull it?" I directed the question at Austin since he appeared calmer at the moment.

"No, unless there is a surveillance camera showing the fire alarm box, which I doubt."

"Are you on drugs or just finally lost your mind?" Em continued.

"Let's get into one of the restaurants, and I'll tell you everything," I said. I glanced behind us one last time to be sure that I didn't see anyone following.

The city block housed at least a half dozen restaurants, the kind that post their menu in the window. We darted into the nearest one without looking to determine if we liked the food. Austin got us a table and I scooted into my seat, warily glancing around in my paranoid state.

"Spill it, all of it." Em had stopped looking shocked with that round "o" of a mouth, and now she just looked mad. Or scared.

The waiter stood patiently, waiting for us to acknowledge him. He began handing out the menus and looked to me first as I was focused on him.

I looked up. "I'd like a Coke, please."

"And what will you have, Miss?" he said to Em. She continued to stare at me with the determination of a dog fixated on his favorite bone. Without looking up, she said, "I'll have a sweet tea."

Austin ordered a drink and a large order of nachos for us to share. He sat back in his chair and folded his arms. "I'm ready to hear the details myself."

Em caught the word "details" immediately. "So, you know something about all this? If my mother catches wind of this, I'm dead. And she'll be calling your dad to let him know that his daughter is a delinquent troublemaker." She put as much dramatic emphasis into the phrase "delinquent troublemaker" as possible.

I looked at the faces of my best friends. You have to trust somebody in this world, right? That person used to be Pete. I had to protect my dad from this. After losing his wife and son, this tidbit might drive him off the deep end. If I couldn't trust my best buds, I might as well give up and go with the crew cut twins.

I just hoped they didn't decide to lock me in a padded room after hearing the story.

***

Austin had leaned forward attentively and Em sat wide-eyed in awe of my details outlining the origins of Regulus and Arizona. The waiter had brought an enormous platter of nachos that slowly disappeared as I talked while Em and Austin ate. I left out some of the details like the appearance of Regulus and Arizona in my garage and the subsequent semi-kidnapping in my own home. And I made a split-second decision to leave out the part about me being some gifted portal detecting human. As if I even knew what that implied...

I was amazed that they didn't seem to question the dimensional portal like I imagined that they would have. Even though I knew that my story was the gospel truth, I wondered just how much the National Enquirer had desensitized them to out-of-this-world sightings.

"I knew that those guys were freaks. No doubt in my mind," Austin said while nodding his head as if it all made sense now.

I just ignored Austin's self-affirmation. "The point is, Pete is involved in this. But something went wrong today. People were after me. Or after Pete. And I'm not sure if they are IIA or not, but I have to assume. And I feel bad for Dr. Bleeker...and I don't know if my own house will be safe when I get home."

Em looked thoughtful as she picked nachos with only her favorite ingredients off the plate. She looked up at me and spoke just barely above a whisper, "So, you're sure that Pete was there today?"

I knew that she was treading carefully here. She, of all people, knew how much I had to believe that I would see my brother again.

"Yes," I stated with no hesitation or doubt.

"Why?" Austin was always the bolder of my two friends. He didn't say it in a challenging or "prove it" manner, but he let me know that he needed to know.

"I picked up a penny and a business card from the table," I answered. "I'm not positive about the card, because right now it doesn't mean anything to me, but I know he left the penny."

"Anybody could have stuck a penny there, Mia. They aren't hard to come by," he said in a let-her-down gently voice. "What does the penny mean? Why would Pete leave it?"

"Pete and I always played hide-and-seek in the house when we were little. I could never find Pete. He was actually pretty good at hiding, and I was pretty bad at finding. Anyway, he would carry pennies in his pocket and leave a trail of pennies as hints for me to find him. I knew I was on the right track if I found a penny."

"You think the penny is to tell you that you're on the right trail and he's still hiding," Em said with a sympathetic look on her face.

That look just set me off. "Look, you guys, either you believe me or you don't. I'm not crazy. Maybe both of you are crazy because you can doubt that Pete is out there, but you don't hesitate to believe that travelers from another dimension are hanging out in my woods waiting to catch dimension criminals like Dr. Bleeker."

"We've never thought you were crazy." Austin covered my hand with his.

Em noticed immediately, and I drew my hand back from the table.

Austin continued, "We need to know all the facts to help you figure this out."

"Mia, if you're crazy then we'll be crazy with you," Em said, smiling. "That's what best friends do. You've always been there for me."

Two years ago when Pete had disappeared, Em had been secretly diagnosed with anorexia. Secretly because Mrs. Peggy Sue didn't want it to be public knowledge that her daughter had an eating disorder. Em's dad knew and I knew. That's it. Peggy Sue had a long talk with me about my responsibilities as a friend to watch over Em. I didn't care what Mrs. Peggy Sue thought I should be doing. I knew that I didn't want my friend to starve herself to death. I was there for Em because I was her best friend, not for her mother's sake.

"How do we go back to the hotel tonight now that some creepy guys are following me?" I summed up the situation, relieved that I had shared my burden.

Austin pulled out his phone, punched numbers, and smiled as he held the phone to his ear, "Tiny, hey I got another favor... I know, I know, I owe you big time. What can be done about someone stalking my girl here?"

I wasn't thrilled about being called "his girl," but I let it go.

He hung up and turned to me. "Tiny says that the conference has security muscle, and we tell them that you're being harassed. These guys don't work for the hotel, and GameCon wouldn't want the bad publicity of something happening to a teenage girl while here. We just have to do that when we get back, and you won't be able to walk two feet without a bodyguard."

"Who is this Tiny, and who are you? It's like you have these connections."

"Yeah, you need to meet Tiny. I know lots of people outside of Whispering Woods, ya know. You guys really need to broaden your horizons," he said with a smirk.

"I think I've broadened them all I can stand for this week," I said in exasperation.

Em's phone rang, and she answered while mouthing to us that the caller was her mother. I watched my friend placate her mom. Em had learned how to manipulate her, which was a little sad. Actually, it made me appreciate the honest relationship that I had with my dad. That is, honest until last week.

"My mom wants to take us to House of Blues to see live music. Dave Matthews is there, and she doesn't want to go alone."

"Dave Matthews? Really?" Austin seemed amused.

"You know who that is?" Em and I said almost in unison.

"Um...yeah," Austin said.

"Don't tell me that you and Peggy Sue listen to the same music. I'll have officially entered the twilight zone." I grinned.

"Hold on, I didn't say that he's on my playlist. But since I'm feeling a little unsure about going back to the hotel right now, it might be a good thing. If you guys want to go to hear some tunes, I won't leave you at the mercy of a wild and wicked Peggy Sue. Where's your mom right now?" Austin asked Em.

"She hasn't gone back to the hotel yet so she has no idea about the fire alarm. How about I call and say we'll meet her there?"

"Let's blow this joint. Call and tell her we're on our way. Just be sure to tell her that she'll have to behave herself," Austin said as he signaled at the waiter that we needed our ticket. "No going cougar for Mrs. Peggy Sue, and Mia will have to stop herself from picking up any guys from another species."

"Oh, that was so not funny. Mrs. Peggy Sue going cougar..." I shivered.

***

Mrs. Peggy Sue waited impatiently for us in a line outside the club. She wore her colorful, oversize jewelry like a beacon to guide wayward teenagers. She would have been hard to miss.

"Austin, dear, what took you so long? I've been waiting for you."

I looked at Emily to see if we were invisible. Mrs. Peggy Sue had been happily married, several times. She was on husband number four. I truly hoped the newest husband understood that Mrs. Peggy Sue loved men. All men.

"We hit a little afternoon traffic. This isn't Whispering Woods, you know." Austin draped one arm around my back and the other around Em's as if to pull us into the conversation.

Mrs. Peggy Sue was smiling prettily at Austin. "You sure haven't stopped growing, Austin," she said as her eyes traveled from the top of his head down to his feet. "You are definitely filling out."

I glanced sideways at Austin. What was the woman talking about? Mrs. Peggy Sue wasn't leering as much as appreciating. She just noticed things about men.

"Mother..." Em muttered just loud enough for me to catch as her cheeks turned pink.

"Hey, do we need to get our tickets?" I asked.

"I've got them." She waved them like a fan. "I called ahead after I hung up with Emily and reserved our tickets."

"Why are we in this line if we already have tickets?" I asked her.

"This is the line to get in, hon." Mrs. Peggy Sue pulled on my arm to situate me in the line behind her. The couple behind me gave me a dirty look. She saw it immediately and looked at the young man unflinchingly in the eyes. "They were supposed to be here earlier, but you know how kids are. Always running late. You two are sure a cute couple. Do you have children?"

The man shifted uncomfortably and shook his head. He avoided looking at the pretty brunette beside him. I guessed that they were probably just on a date. And they probably wished that they weren't in line behind Mrs.

Peggy Sue.

"I am so sorry." Em looked apologetically at the couple. "We can go to the back of the line."

"No, that's OK. We don't mind," said the brunette.

"We wouldn't want you to split up."

I looked to the end of the line that was growing longer by the minute. "Thanks, that's…" I stopped in mid-sentence. At the end of a string of enthusiastic fans waiting to hear some live music from their favorite band stood Mr. Crew Cut. He stood with his arms folded looking like a bouncer at a rowdy event.

Mr. Crew Cut nodded at me without breaking eye contact. Austin hugged my shoulders reassuringly. I understood that he had seen the same look of acknowledgement from the man.

"That was for us, right?" Austin continued to stare at the man as if it were a contest to see who would look away first.

"For me, Austin. This isn't about you and Em." I could hear Mrs. Peggy Sue's voice droning in the background about the mall she had canvassed for bargains all day while we were at GameCon. Em was trapped in the conversation with her mom, but she glanced suspiciously from me to Austin, fully aware of the tension that sat like a cloud around us.

Austin pulled out his phone and started talking while he stared at the man in an unwavering challenge. "Tiny, hey man. If I tell you the dude's name, can you look up his profile on the registration list? Sure, yeah, I know, I know." Austin jammed his cell phone back into his jeans pocket.

The line was moving quicker now and we were within twenty feet of the man. He wasn't taking his eyes off me. He had that military look, all hard lines seaming a face that hadn't cracked a smile in this decade. I wondered how Austin was going to get his name.

The man turned to fish out his cell phone and make a call. And then I saw it.

Unbelievable. Mr. Crew Cut had forgotten to take off the nametag that was a requirement for admission into the GameCon rooms. Em, Austin, and I had removed ours as soon as we had started walking outside the convention center toward the restaurant.

We would be close enough to touch the guy in minutes, and I still didn't have a plan. If they could follow me this well, then I figured that I was out of luck.

The man shoved his phone back in his jacket pocket and turned away. Within seconds, he slipped into the crowd outside House of Blues and vanished. Something had happened in that phone call, but I wasn't sure what.

"He went to the parking lot," Austin whispered. "But I got his name."

"That was too weird. Why follow us all over the city and give up when we are right in front of him?" I tried to keep my voice low, but Mrs. Peggy Sue wouldn't have heard anyway. She was busy chattering to the people in line behind. I gave the couple a consoling smile.

"Maybe they don't like rock music." Em smiled weakly. "The other one left, too. I noticed another man fitting the description you gave during dinner. He had been hanging around staring at us from about twenty people back and now he's gone."

I was impressed that Em had been so observant. I shouldn't have been surprised. Em was the type who could survey a crowd then describe every person in it. She noticed things like clothes, hair color, and height. She made a heck of an eyewitness. Or a pretty good friend when you're on the run from who knows what. It felt good to have friends watching my back. I stuck my hand in my right hip pocket and fingered the card and penny.

***

After spending the night at the hotel with Em's mom, I was ready to leave. Peggy Sue acted like she was having the time of her life in her slumber party delusions. Maybe the woman lacked friends of her own, but I didn't want to talk about dating and clothes. Please spare me if this is what having a mother was like, I thought.

I had the evidence that I needed from GameCon. Pete was definitely sending me messages. However, Austin had arranged a meeting with Tiny before we were to head home.

***

"She isn't wanted by the cops or anything," Austin reassured Tiny for the third time. "But some guys are following her."

Tiny was a hulking giant wearing a knit toboggan hat and a hockey shirt. Red, curly hair peeked out from the edges of his cap and freckles smattered across his nose gave him the look of an innocent, oversize kid.

"I don't know what you're getting me into, you moron," He said while pacing furiously across the two-foot space at the end of his hotel room bed. "As soon as I used that name for a search in all my usual databases, my software detected a tail on my search. Do you know how improbable that is? That someone is monitoring my activity?"

So much for first impressions. He pulled off his toboggan cap and ran his fingers through his curly mop, damp with perspiration. He stopped pacing and sat down, dwarfing the hotel's desk chair and barely squeezing between the armrests. He replaced the black toboggan and took a deep breath.

I looked at Austin, who for once looked unsure of himself, then met Tiny's stare. "Listen, I'm in deep," I said. "This isn't something with the local authorities or anything like that. This is much bigger. This is sort of like Big Brother, if you know what I mean."

"Wow, you're impressing me with your analytical acrobatics." Tiny mocked me. "I'm good at what I do. If someone has hacked into my system, then it's someone better than me. And that is hard to do." He stated it as a fact rather than opinion.

"We won't ask you for help again. Sorry to get you into this." I started to leave. Em, standing near the door, opened it.

"Whoa, hold up." Tiny rose from the chair. "You guys can't cut me out now. I just didn't know the level of what we were dealing with here. You should have prepared me. Next time, you gimme the lowdown."

I stopped and stared at Tiny. Austin, who had been following me out, nearly ran into me. The small room looked smaller with Tiny standing.

"This isn't fun and games. I appreciate your help with the flash mob thing and looking up that guy, but I don't want to get you into any trouble."

"You underestimate my skills. Austin's my friend, and if he says you need our help, then my investigative skills are at your service. I watch out for my bros. And I'd like to hear about why The Man is after you. You seem pretty harmless to me."

"Thanks, Tiny." Austin shook his hand and bumped knuckles. Austin's head didn't even reach Tiny's chin in height. It's good that the hotel room had high ceilings.

Em's cell played the ring tone I recognized. Mrs. Peggy Sue was checking up on her. Again, for the third time since we had entered Tiny's hotel room.

"Helicopter mom again?" Tiny smirked.

I raised my eyebrows at Austin since I had no clue what that meant. Austin waited till Em was talking to her mom and couldn't hear. "It means she's a micromanager," Austin whispered.

"Thanks, Tiny. We need to go," I said. "Em's mom is probably ready to leave and wants Em to check out with her."

"Watch your back," Tiny said. "I'll be in touch."

***

Austin and I drove home in silence. Talking was difficult with the Jeep top off. I was glad. Leaves were beginning to turn red and gold and the weather was mild. It would have been a beautiful time for a drive if I didn't have so much on my mind. Mrs. Peggy Sue had insisted that we continue to drive together for safety purposes. I could see her Suburban in the rear view mirror. She was attempting to keep up with Austin who was not thrilled at being tethered to Em's mom on the trip home.

Near Whispering Woods, the Suburban finally turned off to go its separate route and we continued toward my house. When Austin drove onto my gravel drive, he glanced at me several times, as though he had something to say and didn't know how to say it.

"Spit it out, Austin." I leaned my head back against the seat and took a deep breath.

"Is your dad home tonight?"

"He said he will be home. Quit worrying. I will turn on the alarm system until he gets home if he's not already in there. You just be careful going home. If they know about Tiny helping me, then they are watching you for sure."

"I'll wait if your dad isn't home."

"No, you aren't my bodyguard."

"No, I'm not. A bodyguard watches out for somebody as a job. I'm your friend, and I care about you. I need to know that you're safe."

We had reached the house, and Austin shut the motor off. I was going to jump out and get my bag but Austin set his hand on my shoulder. "I know you think this is all about finding Pete, but it's not. There is more going on here than we know. I don't want to lose you. I don't want you to disappear."

I laid my hand on top of his. "I know that. I feel better knowing that you and Em are helping me figure this out. I also feel guilty about that."

"Safety in numbers. Two heads are better than one.

Three heads will figure this out. Four, counting Tiny." As it turned out, my dad hadn't made it in yet. Austin insisted on checking every closet and cranny in the house before waiting while I set the alarm system. I pulled the curtain back and saw Austin hesitate on my front porch with his back to me. He was looking into the woods. Finally, he jumped into his Jeep and drove away.

I hauled my bag up the stairs and sorted through the clothes on my bedroom floor to start on laundry and homework. With all the drama lately, I was getting behind in my classes. My phone rang with the standard ring tone, meaning that it wasn't my dad or friends. I looked at the display and didn't recognize the number. I didn't answer it, so it went to voicemail. I waited for the beep signaling that I had a message and checked. "Mia, I need your help. Now. I know you're home. Call back, please." I recognized Arizona's voice. He sounded funny. Shaken.

Maybe I needed Arizona and Regulus for information about Pete. Or maybe not. Now that I was sure that Pete had contacted me, I should stay as far away from them as possible. Pete had warned me about them, hadn't he? Trust no one... And then Dr. Bleeker had told me about the

IIA taking his wife. The kicker, of course, was that the IIA had followed me to Dallas. Did they think that because the IIA agents weren't Arizona and Regulus that I wouldn't notice?

I heard a noise from downstairs. I rushed out of my bedroom and stood on the landing so I could see the entire entry way into my house. I could tell that the noise was on the front porch.

Biscuit started to bark at the front door. Who needed an alarm system when you had Biscuit?

The banging on the front door was immediate and insistent. I ran downstairs and was glad that the person outside couldn't see me. I peeked out of the peephole.

Arizona stood too close to the peephole, trying to look through it from his side. He backed away from the door. I could see the distorted peephole glass image of Arizona's large head and smaller body. Behind him and off the porch, I could also make out something on the ground.

On a blanket, Regulus lay still. That is, I assumed the body was Regulus. I couldn't tell due to the dark red substance that marred his features.

He was covered in blood.

Chapter Thirteen

Trap

There are two kinds of people in the world: those who watch out for themselves, and those who feel the need to help others. I guess I fall into that second category, whether I like it or not. I stared for exactly five more seconds before my instincts took over and I opened the door.

"What happened to him?" I ran out and closed the door behind me.

Biscuit had managed to squeeze out before I could stop him and ran over to what I could now see was a tarp. He started to lick Regulus's face and ears. "No!" I scolded.

Regulus didn't move. I squatted down on my haunches and grabbed his wrist, checking for a pulse. I found it hard to breathe as I got a closer look.

His beautiful face had become a bloodied pulp.

Arizona stood framed by the sunset, watching me with relief on his face. "I knew you would come through on this," he whispered. "I need to get back through the portal. Someone set a trap near it, and Regulus will die if I don't bring back something to counteract the poison. The portal has moved." He grabbed my hand unsteadily. "You can find it. It's still here somewhere close."

I wrenched my hand away, scared. "You can find another one, right?" I avoided his eyes. "You're wrong! I don't know how to do it. You think I'm like some kind of dousing rod, but I'm just me."

"I don't have time to argue with you." His eyes accused me. "I won't allow Regulus to die just because you're too scared to admit you can do it."

"You're wrong." My eyes watered with guilt and shame.

"Take care of my brother while I'm gone."

"Hey, wait a minute. You can't just leave him with me." My voice had reached a high-pitched squeal. "I mean, I have a first aid kit. Maybe we can fix him up with that. Or you can take him with you. If he was poisoned, where did all this blood come from?" I shuddered as I examined Regulus's face and arms and could see tiny puncture wounds. The cuts formed a crisscross pattern across his cheek.

"I'm wasting time. You can make sure he lives. I have to go. I'll explain later."

"Wait! What am I supposed to do with him? My dad will be home any minute. I can't take him in the house. I couldn't get him up the stairs if I wanted to." My pleas fell on deaf ears as Arizona detached the tarp held by ropes to the back of his motorcycle and left.

I looked at his retreating back with dismay. Biscuit whined at my feet, clearly distressed as he paced back and forth at the edge of the tarp. Now that Arizona was out of sight, what was I supposed to do? I glanced down at the ropes that Arizona had removed from his bike. I tugged one with each hand. Leaning back with my full weight, I tried to use some physics to pull the tarp across the grass. It shifted a centimeter.

Regulus twitched and his eyes fluttered. Until that movement, I had assumed that he was unconscious. I knelt down to him, nudging Biscuit away from Regulus's head. "Listen, I don't know if you can hear me. But I'm going to have to move you. And then... I don't know what. Hang on. Arizona went to get help for you."

Regulus's eyes opened into thin slits, and I could see that he was trying to focus. His lips opened but nothing came out. I remembered the golf cart and realized I could use it to move him. I rose and almost jumped out of my skin when a hand reached out to grab my wrist.

I looked at his hand. Blood had formed outlines around his nails.

He attempted to speak and it came out as a weak croak. "Don't leave me. Please."

"I'm coming right back. I'm getting the golf cart to pull you."

"I can't have you."

I looked at him, startled as I tried to decode what that meant. I yanked my wrist free. "I don't have time to listen to you talking out of your head. Let me move you and figure out what first aid stuff I might remember from health class."

I ran to the garage and drove the golf cart over as close to him as possible. The rope ends needed to be secure if I were going to drag some weight on the tarp, so I thought about the knots I could do. Who would ever guess that tagging along with an older brother to Boy Scouts might actually come in handy one day? I'd learned the knots quicker than Pete had.

I visually pictured one of the knots called a clove hitch. I wound both ropes' ends in a figure eight around the bumper and then back up through itself again. After I tied both ropes, I looked down at Regulus. He looked strangely like a puffer fish. His face and hands were swollen and red underneath the coating of dried blood.

The golf cart pulled the tarp and passenger, sliding on the grass and I wheeled slowly around to the back of the house. A large deck framed the back of our log house with a view of the valley to the west. Underneath the decking supported by large timber posts, a person would have to search the darkness to see the door that led to a basement room. I never came down here. I preferred the light airy atmosphere of my room with the view of the world outside.

I ran over to the unused backyard fire pit. Beneath a cement block, I found the key that Pete had hidden for quick use. He had hated getting a key from my dad and had ferreted away the extra that he proceeded to call "our secret key." I unlocked and opened the door, glancing back at Regulus. He hadn't moved since he had grabbed my wrist. With my adrenaline surging, I fell back on the ground when I managed to pull the tarp across the threshold and inside to safety.

***

"Don't move."

He jerked his head from side to side and tried to sit up.

"I said, don't move." I eased his head back to the pillow on the floor.

I'd tried to drag him away from the doorway, but I couldn't drag him around when furniture and stuff was everywhere. By stuff, I mean miscellaneous remnants of a life I could barely remember. The basement was a carpeted room with harsh manmade lighting throwing jagged shadows against the cinderblock walls. Once, the plan had been to finish it as a room or studio. Pete had imagined that it would be his private jam studio for the garage band he'd hoped to form someday. I'd been told that my mother had dreamed of making pottery here and a potter's wheel sat in a corner as evidence.

Squished in the middle of all this lay Regulus.

I replaced the ice packs on his face and arms. After careful examination, it looked as though something had touched or cut into his skin and caused it to swell. None of his cuts were deep; they were suspiciously shallow. They formed a pattern that left me curious as to what had inflicted the damage.

"Open your mouth." I slid my hand under his head to lift it.

A look of panic crossed his face. He stared and met my eyes. He nodded as if he had made a decision.

I held a tablespoon of Benadryl to his mouth and forced him to slowly part his lips to take in the liquid.

Dad's voice sounded in my memories. *Vicks VapoRub and Benadryl, cures for all that ails you.*

I knew that a simple antihistamine would help the swelling, but I had no background in emergency medical treatment. If I could get to my laptop, maybe I could search for a remedy. The problem was that he didn't look that hurt. I knew he wasn't faking unconsciousness. And he had definitely been out of it.

I realized that he was staring back at me.

"I can't tell what's wrong with you, and Arizona went somewhere. I mean, I can see that you have a pattern of cuts and your skin is swelling around that pattern. I'm trying to get the swelling down. You have to help me. Tell me what to do."

"Where am I?" Regulus whispered, looking around the room and probably not seeing much from his angle. "You're in my house." His brows furrowed.

"In the basement. We never use it except for more storage."

His muscles visibly relaxed, but his eye contact was more intense than ever. "What do you think of me?" The question came out urgent and breathless.

I ignored the question. "What happened to you? What made these marks?"

"A biological weapon. A web."

"What do you mean, a web. Like a spider web?"

"Maybe the trap was an arachnid's web, or maybe some other creature."

I tried not to roll my eyes at his substitute of arachnid for spider. I had never seen a spider's web that left marks or for that matter even hurt.

"This poisonous...arachnid...built a web that you're allergic to?"

"Someone set this trap near the portal. This creature is not of your world. There is no way that it journeyed here without being transported by a higher level species. Humans brought it and hid it there to deliver its poison."

"The Slips did this?"

He gave me a funny look. He closed his eyes and seemed to be exhausted after talking so much. "We are not sure who put it there." His skin was taking on an odd shade of purple. The planes of his face were beginning to bruise in addition to the swelling.

I tried not to panic.

He grabbed my hand, "Did you arrange the trap?"

"I've been gone, so no, and I wouldn't try to hurt you anyways. And didn't you send those two thugs to follow me?"

I sensed relief as he sighed. "I would follow you. I would not send others." He began to cough.

The bags of ice were melting, so fresh ice packs were the next order of business. I looked at my watch. How long had Arizona been gone? An hour? Less? "I'm going upstairs to fill an ice chest and bring it down here."

He didn't respond, so I ran to accomplish my task as quickly as possible. Upstairs, I discovered that my dad still wasn't home. I checked my cell phone for messages. Delayed in Atlanta's airport, Dad wouldn't be home until tomorrow. And tomorrow would be a college campus visit day for seniors. Sometimes the stars do align after all.

***

The silence of the room was maddening. Silence except for the clock. The *tick, tick, tick* sounded like a voice scolding, "Time, time, time is wasting away." The low rhythmic sound bled out into my head into a brown blanket of color tinged in warm gold. I was tired. Even Biscuit had curled up next to Regulus's knee and fallen asleep.

Arizona had been gone for at least two hours.

I searched the canvas bag of snacks I'd packed from a trip to the kitchen. An outsider might guess that I planned to be down here through a nuclear holocaust, judging by the amount of goods I had in front of me. I opened a package of peanut butter crackers as quietly as I could but saw Regulus's eyes flutter at the sound. I couldn't tell if he opened his eyes or not. They looked swollen now and firmly closed. Or would the swelling make it more difficult to open them?

"Go ahead and eat," he said in a croaky, low voice.

"Sorry," I said tersely. "I was hungry. Are you hungry? Arizona will be back any minute now. I have all kinds of things in this bag. I don't know what you like. I have crackers, nacho cheese chips, some baby carrots..."

He interrupted my babbling by shaking his head in a negative response. "Talk to me. It helps if I hear you talking."

"Oh," I said lamely.

He barely opened his eyes and looked at my face. I turned my head and looked over his shoulder, uncomfortable. Biscuit opened his eyes and set his furry chin on Regulus's knee. The dog looked so at home with Regulus, as though he knew that Regulus was hurt and needed the comfort of a touch. I, on the other hand, felt useless. Useless because he didn't ask for much. Just talk. I couldn't think of a thing to say.

After hearing the ticking of the clock for another minute, Regulus whispered, "Why do you love Pete?"

I wondered at the strangeness of the question.

"Because he's my brother."

"Do all brothers and sisters love each other?"

I hesitated, thinking about that. "Probably not. It might depend on if they were raised in the same house and if they get along. But I think you have to feel something for your family, even if you don't like them. But I do love Pete as much as I love my dad."

He nodded as if satisfied with the answer. He winced.

"Do you have any brothers or sisters?" I asked, hoping to distract him from the pain.

"Only Arizona."

"But he's not really your brother, right?" I took a fresh ice pack from the cooler and carefully arranged it on his neck.

"No. No brother, no parents."

"Everyone has parents. You're saying that you don't know them."

"I have Makers, not parents."

"What does that mean? Makers?"

I waited for a response as I listened to the steady

click of the clock. I looked at his face painted with purple and red swollen flesh and was dismayed at how different he looked. Regulus was quite possibly the most attractive guy I had ever seen in person. This swollen face belonged to a stranger. He never answered, and I felt beyond demanding to satisfy my morbid curiosity.

He startled me by reaching for my hand as he arched his back and moaned. I let him take my hand. "It'll be OK when Arizona gets back," I cooed in the voice you would use with a child while stroking his hair with my free hand. He loosened his grip.

What was taking Arizona so long?

My cell phone ring tone, "Wild Thing," played indicating that Austin was calling. Austin had a habit of sneakily reprogramming my ring tone to suit him.

"That's Austin. I need to answer."

Regulus tried to sit up, panicking at my words. I could see his familiar blue eyes as he made eye contact and said, "No, please, no."

"I have to answer. He'll just come over here if I don't. Besides, he knows everything now. He and Emily both do." I breathed out heavily, glad to have made the confession.

Regulus lay back and stared at the ceiling, not saying a word and not looking at me. I felt the horrible guilt of seeing his face at my words. Even in its disfigured state, I could tell how much the confession scared him. I was surprised to think about him being scared.

"They won't tell anyone. I promise. I was afraid. I thought that you had sent those guys to follow me to

Dallas. I didn't know what else to do."

"Maybe they can protect you," he stated in a flat voice, "I cannot protect myself or you."

"I'm fine. And I'm not letting anything happen to you. This room is like a fortress. See the deadbolts? I guess you can't, but nobody is getting in here." I squeezed his hand. "Trust me."

I knew I sounded brave, but I was coming to realize that the thugs in Dallas were news to him. He rubbed his thumb over the top of my hand and it reminded me of the way a person rubs a worry stone.

I disengaged my hand and picked up my cell phone. After texting Austin that I would call him back in a little while, I asked, "You didn't try to follow me this weekend after I talked to Dr. Bleeker?"

"We were called to the Vault," he answered.

"What's the Vault?"

"It is the information center. The IIA headquarters are there. They sent for Arizona and me. We were required to return for further instructions and updates. It seems that Dr. Bleeker has been a busy man. Bleeker has been leaving a trail of dead bodies across four of your districts...states."

"Dead bodies? Not Dr. Bleeker. That can't be right. Why would he kill someone?" I couldn't imagine that the information was correct. There had to be a mistake.

"It may be unintentional. We do not know, but we can guess that he has been using people from other worlds as test subjects. He fled his own world to conduct illegal experiments."

"Oh, God. He's like a mad scientist. And a murderer.

I didn't know what was at stake. I didn't understand." Horrified, I covered my face with my hands.

He reached for my hands, took them in both of his. "He offers hope to the hopeless. He has been creating a specific virus for gene therapy. He creates the virus in a lab and injects it into his subject. It's a more effective delivery than chemical vector delivery, but easily contaminated. His goal is to alter DNA, but he's failing and causing his subjects' deaths. The IIA doesn't think that the general population has been exposed to viral contamination yet... What happened to you while we were gone?" His grip loosened.

"Austin, Em, and I went to a convention in Dallas. I thought Pete would be there, but that's another story. These two guys were definitely following me. They didn't try to act like they weren't."

"Did they harm you?" His eyes were intense despite his swollen lids.

"No way. I was just scared. I mean, I wasn't scared for myself, but for Em and Austin...and well, Dr. Bleeker."

His hand shifted to touch my knee as if to reassure himself that I wasn't going anywhere. I rested one of my hands over the top of his.

"You were the only one in danger. They didn't want the others. Why were you frightened for Dr. Bleeker?" I confessed all that Dr. Bleeker had said to me in the student center.

"Dr. Bleeker has broken the laws of man and nature. You can't get in the way. You are important, but not indispensable."

"Listen, I get it that you feel some sort of

responsibility for me. Right now, you need to quit worrying about me."

My cell phone starting ringing. An ordinary ring tone, not "Wild Thing."

"Mia, it's me. Where are you?" Arizona's voice.

"Come to the back of the house. There's a door at the back left corner. It's almost hidden under the deck," I said, and then added, "Hurry!"

I let go of Regulus's hand and felt cold. I didn't realize how warm and feverish his hand had been.

I heard insistent rapping and opened the door. I hugged Arizona in relief.

"Did he make it?"

"What do you mean, did he make it? Did you think he was going to die?" My voice sounded shrill and echoed through the basement. "I've been going crazy not knowing what to do with him." I pulled Arizona by the hand around the furniture and boxes to the place where I had hidden Regulus.

"How did you get him over here?" He sounded amazed.

"I cleared the stuff to make a path and pulled him on a blanket. Moving him wasn't easy." I shrugged. "Now what?"

Arizona pulled a small box out of his pocket and removed a small square of translucent paper. He bent and set his thumb on Regulus's bottom lip. "Open up, friend. I need to put this on your tongue."

Regulus closed his eyes, meekly allowing the paper to dissolve on his tongue. The purple bruising started to recede, and his face molded into its normal shape in seconds.

"Oh, my gosh, that's incredible." I couldn't hide my

excitement. The tension of the last hour faded in the pure bliss of knowing Regulus would be OK.

"The alchemist was slow, but she did well." Arizona examined the marks on Regulus's face as they magically disappeared. "It's against law for me to bring him back through after he was contaminated."

Regulus sat up and grabbed my arms. "You have to take us to Dr. Bleeker, now. He's coming after you."

Arizona's mouth set in a straight, hard line. "The poisonous webbing was across your front door, Mia."

"What do you mean? I've gone through that door today." I was confused.

"I cleared the door immediately. If I hadn't, you would be like Regulus is now." Arizona looked me in the eyes. "The stakes are always high in our life. Don't fool yourself that we're playing games."

I was stunned. I had assumed that the trap had been set at the mouth of the portal. The implications of a death trap across my door shocked me. It could have killed me or even worse, my dad. Why would Dr. Bleeker want to get rid of me?

I flashed back to the Regulus of only an hour ago and shuddered. I lifted my head in guilt. "Tell me what to do."

"Call Austin. We could use someone to help watch out for you," Regulus said. I saw a funny look pass between Arizona and Regulus. The moment passed, and we had to move before Bleeker did.

Chapter Fourteen

Dead Slips

The flickering of the lab lights made me nauseous. Why couldn't the university replace the fluorescent bulb when lighting was this bad? I stopped the complaints going through my head when I remembered that I was a trespasser. Breaking and entering doesn't leave you room to be demanding.

"Can we go now? Regulus doesn't look well yet and Dr. Bleeker's obviously gone." I hated to sound whiny, but it was the middle of the night. Austin looked amazingly content, despite the late hour, at having been included in the escapade and tasked with watching me. His calm demeanor was annoying.

"Yeah, he's about as useful as a pogo stick in quicksand." Austin stared at Regulus.

Regulus straightened from leaning on the laboratory workstation. A fine sheen of sweat gave his face a shiny glow. His black hair clung to his head with soft curls edging his neckline.

Arizona glanced at Regulus, apparently assessing his physical condition, and shook his head. "Something isn't right. Why would Bleeker go to so much trouble to set a trap for you and then leave?" Arizona asked.

"We need to search every area he had access to," Regulus said. "What about that door at the back?"

"Looks like a supply closet to me." I started to leave the room.

Regulus went slowly toward the door. I ran over to help him, but he shrugged me off as if embarrassed. A second later, I saw a strange look on his face and he braced his arm around my shoulders to steady himself as we walked the final steps to the door. I looked up to see Austin scowling.

Regulus took a small tool from his pocket and stuck the rod into the key lock. The door lock clicked, and he quickly turned the knob. My eyes adjusted to the blackness of the supply room with its shelves filled with microscopes, glassware, and chemicals. Then I looked down.

I screamed.

Regulus slapped his hand over my mouth to muffle my high-pitched reaction, and I almost fell. Austin backed away from the door in disbelief.

Arizona dropped to his knees to set his fingers on the young woman's throat to check for a pulse, but it wasn't necessary. Her face was bloated and her eyes stared straight ahead. She was propped up in a sitting position with her arms hanging limply at her sides.

I saw the bundle beside her on the floor. A silky

wisp of black hair peeked out of the cloth.

Regulus shoved in front of me. "Don't look. You shouldn't see this," he whispered. He took my chin and lifted it, forcing me to look into his eyes.

I heard Austin's voice, "He's right, Mia. You don't want to see this."

I nodded my head, stunned at the horror. I'd seen more than just a dead woman.

"Hey dude, what do you think you're doing? Isn't this where we call 911?" Austin held up his cell phone, ready.

"No policemen, Austin," answered Arizona. "How do you think you'll explain this? This woman is not of this world, nor is the child. Dr. Bleeker has left his mess for us to clean up."

"And he killed them?" My voice came out as a croak.

I blinked hard at hearing the truth about Dr. Bleeker for the second time today.

"Bleeker believed in life and healing, but he couldn't follow the rules. His own misfortunes in life have distorted his reality of what is right." Arizona's voice held no emotion.

Austin stared at us as if he had grasped the enormity of the situation. "So now what?"

"We bury them. Isn't that normal?" Arizona looked exasperated.

"Normal. Normal?" Austin's voice had risen. He rubbed his hand over his forehead. Afraid, he was hiding his face.

"Hey, Austin. It's gonna be OK." I removed myself from the warmth of Regulus's arms. I hadn't even realized that I had hidden my face in his chest for comfort. "We need some big trash bags. Come on. We don't have all night." Even though I was shaking the words came out evenly.

They stared.

"I don't know which is scarier: dead people in the closet or you taking charge of the cover-up," Austin said with a nervous laugh.

Regulus started and suddenly smiled. He said cheerfully, "You heard her. Find something to wrap them up and I'll watch the entrance."

I turned my head away from the closet and began opening doors at the bottom of each lab station. Austin disappeared, then showed up a few minutes later holding a large roll of heavy fabric. "Here's a tarp I keep in my Jeep."

The three worked together to roll out the tarp near the supply closet door. I went to the lab doorway. "I'll open doors when it's time," I said, embarrassed because I didn't want to touch the bodies. Gutsy one minute, a quivering coward the next.

Austin had met us at the lab in his Jeep, so we had the dilemma of which vehicle could better carry the body, my small car or his Jeep. Two guys carrying a rolled tarp was conspicuous enough. Plus, it was the middle of the night. Austin and Arizona carried the roll with Regulus supporting the middle weight as much as he was able. I stood fidgeting from foot to foot as they struggled with boosting the tarp and its dreadful weight into the Jeep's back seat. Again, I turned away at the sight.

"You go with Austin. Mia and I are going to Bleeker's home in case he went back there." Regulus yelled to Arizona while he jumped into the driver's seat of my car.

"I can drive, you know. I'm fine," I said quietly as I got into the passenger side. I saw Austin backing up to leave.

"We don't want to ask for any more trouble than we have at the moment," he said, turning toward me from the driver's seat. "There's a university security guard coming this way."

"Crap! Why didn't you say so?" I said, panicky.

"Because you were doing beautifully until now. You'll be great as an enforcer. "

"You're so wrong."

Blue and red light flashed behind us. The campus police.

As the police car pulled closer, Regulus edged over the console in the middle. "I hope this works." Leaning over, he surprised me by cupping my face in his hands. I opened my mouth to protest, ask him what he was talking about.

He came even closer. I felt as gooey as a chocolate bar left in a hot car. My insides trembled. He set his lips on mine.

I had been kissed before. Sure I had. Awkwardly, quickly, probing. But I had never felt as though the guy tasted my mouth. But that's exactly what Regulus's kiss felt like. One tentative nibble led to a bigger one and he was diving in.

The pressure of his lips was warm and soft. His tongue slid over my bottom lip and sent tremors and heat from my head to the ends of my toes. My hands wound around his neck to pull him over closer onto my body, to my side of the car. I saw a myriad of colors, plum and red swirling in my delirious mind.

I wanted only to be closer.

A quick and extremely loud rapping sounded right in my ear. It took me a minute to realize that the sound was at the car window. Oh…my…gosh. I had lost my mind. I had forgotten about the campus police, forgotten about the mess we were trying to cover up, had practically forgotten my name in a matter of seconds.

Regulus leaned back to his side and pushed the button to roll down the window. He was a better actor than I could have guessed. He actually looked embarrassed. "Officer? Sorry about that. We didn't hear you come up," he said.

"Yes, son. That's obvious. Do you know that you can't be loitering in the parking lots here at night? Campus ordinance." The officer flashed the light he held in my eyes.

"Yes, sir. We had a late night study session and my friends dropped us off here, at my girlfriend's car." Regulus looked over at me with a shy grin on his face and back at the officer. "We were leaving. I wanted to say goodnight before I take her home."

"Then do so, and don't let me catch you in this lot again. The student lots are in the west corner of the campus." He turned the black flashlight off and clipped it in a belt holster.

"No, sir. I have to get her home immediately. She's past her curfew anyway," Regulus said with a defeated tone.

The officer grinned sympathetically at him and nodded. After he returned to his car, he waited for us to back up and leave the lot.

"OK, was that really necessary?" I shouted. "I don't

think being an enforcer requires being violated by your partner." I folded my arms over my chest. I tried to slow down, but the words came out in a rush like my breath. My heart pounded as adrenaline made me lightheaded.

"I'd do it again, if we weren't in such a hurry," he said in a low confident voice without even looking at me.

"Oh, you would, would you? Well, I..." I lost my train of thought. My face burned. I turned to watch the trees as they whirred past the window.

I would love to be kissed again. How ridiculous. I had dead Slips, a brother hiding out for some reason, a man I trusted trying to kill me, and now a guy who had me wrapped around his little finger. At least that one part felt good.

***

The house sat at the end of the street in an old neighborhood in Whispering Woods. Its tan siding, black shutters, neatly manicured lawn, and iron post gas lamp in front yelled respectable to anybody.

Not to me.

I saw a picture of deceit. A charming lair for the man who had fooled me.

We had parked a block away to observe the house, and I said, "The house is dark. Not even a lamp on. He's already gone."

"It appears that he is," Regulus said. "We need to look around."

"You don't think there's more dead bodies, do you?"

I tried not to squeak. The thought of finding another one made my stomach do a flip. I pictured the dead Slip from the lab and the bundle that I knew to be a baby.

Bile rose in my throat.

"No, I wouldn't assume that. I need to see if I can find any clues of his associates or where he might be going." He glanced at me. "Will you be OK?"

"Sure. Sure." I knew I was repeating myself like an idiot but I had to reassure myself as much as him. I slowly opened the car door.

He glanced at me. "We're going to look around. Five minutes. Then we'll go to meet Arizona and Austin."

He exited the car quietly and I followed. The wind had picked up and lent an appropriate ghostly air to the night. Regulus walked quickly and I concentrated matching his pace. We crossed the neighbor's lawn and stealthily crept to the side door.

Regulus removed an instrument from the pocket of his cargo pants. While he unfolded the gadget, I turned the doorknob. He glanced at me, surprised.

"Unlocked." I gave a tiny push and the door moved.

He grimaced and shoved the tool back into his pocket. He signaled by holding one finger up to indicate that I should wait, and I nodded.

He slid like a fluid cat into the house. I waited with my back pressed to the wall and peered into the darkness inside.

A minute later, he returned and switched on a light.

"You were right. No one's here."

"That makes sense. Who would be walking around in the dark?"

"We were, a few minutes ago," he answered.

I grinned. While walking into Dr. Bleeker's house, an eerie chill traced a path down my spine. The kitchen was bright yellow with pictures covering the refrigerator door panel. Some were taken with a camera and some were drawn by a child. Miscellaneous magnets randomly held them in place. I heard a ticking and looked up to see a clock shaped like a dog over the sink. Its tail wagged back and forth with the clicking sound.

"Homey," I said, looking at Regulus. He'd put gloves on and was opening drawers.

"You may actually be a burglar and I didn't know it. How is it that you have a tool to break into a house...and gloves?"

"Don't touch anything. I'll have to clean your prints off the outer doorknob." He didn't even look up from his task as he said it. "We don't know what other mess Bleeker has left and we don't want you to get blamed for it." He rifled through the drawer of pencils and papers.

"Can I help? I feel kind of useless."

"Look around upstairs but use this to touch anything. We'll take it with us when we leave." He tossed me a kitchen towel. "Look for names of people or places, something that could tell us where he has been or might be going."

"Yeah, I can do that," I said while turning to walk to the staircase. I flipped on the light and then frowned as I looked over my shoulder to see if he was watching. I hurriedly used the cloth to wipe the light switch I'd touched. This was going to be harder than I thought. I wanted my own pair of burglar gloves.

I walked up the staircase quickly before I could lose my nerve. Using the cloth, I switched on the light of the first bedroom I entered and saw race cars decorating the bedding, curtains, and walls. Bookshelves were filled with books and plastic dinosaurs. I had the strange feeling that someone was staring at me and turned to see a row of plastic trolls with bright orange hair on a shelf at eye level. I frowned. I hoped that

Bleeker's kids were OK.

I turned the light out using the cloth and went to the next room. Bingo. I had found the home office. The walls of the office were filled with framed certificates and pictures. I wondered if the certificates were legit or part of this nice picture that he painted for the world to see.

A noise caught my attention, and I stopped what I was doing. Holding my breath, I waited to hear it again. Then I heard the drawers downstairs opening and closing and realized that it must be Regulus in his search.

The desk looked remarkably similar to the one in his office on the campus. There were papers in several stacks that might seem organized to the owner but looked like a mess to me. I clumsily shuffled some papers around with my fingers enveloped in the flour sack material of the kitchen towel. Utility bill, credit card bills, and more bills. A metal letter opener with Mickey Mouse mounted at the top. I wondered if my dad paid these bills every month. I realized that I was ignorant about the running of a household.

I sat and opened the drawer to see the standard pens, paper clips, scissors, and some business cards. I grabbed the cards and shoved them in my jeans pocket.

"Hello. Finding anything interesting?"

In the doorway stood a petite blonde woman pointing a small handgun at me. I noticed the gun first and then her eyes. There was something disturbingly familiar about her. Maybe she worked at the university.

"Don't do anything stupid. You're a smart girl. I want you to stand up and move away from the desk." She spoke the words with an air of confidence while motioning with her head. The gun never wavered.

Rising from the chair, I was startled by a crash sounding from downstairs. I heard Regulus cursing.

She didn't take her eyes off me as she stepped into the hallway. "Gordon," she yelled.

The house was so quiet that I could hear the downstairs clock ticking for a moment.

"Come and get him," Regulus yelled in a strained voice.

Surprise registered on the woman's face and she kept the gun on me while turning her head to look down the stairs. I grabbed the letter opener and tucked it horizontally into the waist of my jeans. Her eyes wandered across the printed words across my chest, "I See Stupid People" and her brow furrowed in a slightly disapproving look.

"You're going to walk down those stairs. Slowly."

She motioned the gun toward the hallway.

How would this end? My mind was racing. But the

fear I had felt earlier was gone, replaced by a determination that I had never experienced before. My mind was clear and certain. Not one sound, color, or thought distracted me as I allowed her to direct my movement down the stairs. One sure foot in front of the other, waiting for the opportunity.

At the bottom of the staircase, I looked into the kitchen to see Regulus standing and holding something pointed at a beefy man who must be Gordon.

Recognition must have been evident on my face before the words left my mouth. "You're the creep from

GameCon."

The woman's gun pressed lightly at the back of my head.

Regulus pushed the silver box against Gordon's temple, the same device that he had used days ago against the Slips. Although I knew that the box could send an electrical shock through a person and disable him, there was something so much more menacing about the thought of a bullet through my brain.

"I'll be sure that this melts his brain tissue. Let her go. It will be a trade." Regulus never looked at me.

He met the woman's eyes with a commanding stare. When she didn't respond, he said, "If we kill them both, it will leave you and me. I'm certain that one of us will die. Who do you think it will be?"

"You won't risk her. You need her." She hesitated like she was thinking it over. The metal of the gun barrel still pressed against my skull.

"Shoot her," Gordon said calmly. A cloud of dark green menace clustered around his head much like a swarm of flies around a carcass.

I forced myself to ignore the vision. "This is like a Mexican standoff."

Regulus stayed silent. He probably had no clue what that meant.

"I have a better idea," the woman said. I wished she'd move the gun. It quivered slightly against my head, and I couldn't tell if she was nervous or getting tired of holding her arm up.

Gordon darted back and, lightning-fast, knocked the silver box from Regulus's hand. It flew through the air and landed ten feet away, sliding across the linoleum floor of the bright yellow kitchen.

I grabbed the letter opener from the waist of my jeans, bent, and stabbed backward. I was blindly hoping to hit something important. I must have succeeded because she screamed and the gun fell away from my head.

Regulus and Gordon were a frenzy of fists before falling to the floor, grappling. They reminded me of the school wrestling team. The woman grabbed the back of my hair. I looked over my shoulder and kicked back frantically. In a move I had seen performed, I then stopped, letting myself fall back against her as she pulled. The momentum of her pulling me landed her on the floor.

I caught myself at the last second and stayed upright. The letter opener was stuck in the woman's thigh and blood poured from the wound. She jerked it out of her leg.

She had dropped the gun, and I grabbed it.

On the floor, Gordon had Regulus in a chokehold. I pointed the gun at Gordon and said, "Let him go. Now, creep." I held the gun steadily with both hands.

When Gordon didn't move, I released the safety, cocked the hammer, and pulled the trigger. A red circle appeared on his sleeve. I had shot him in the upper arm.

He screamed in shock and anger, letting Regulus go. I looked around to see if the woman was coming up behind me. She wasn't. She was gone and the front door was open. Scurrying to his feet, Gordon ran to the side door and left without looking back.

"Please tell me that you've shot a gun before and that wasn't luck," Regulus managed to gasp.

I ran over to help him up. "Sure I have. All the time in *Quest of Zion*. And I've played lots of shooter games."

His eyes widened and he shook his head in disbelief. "Let's get out of here. You are not what you seem, Mia
Taylor."

"I do well under pressure." I shrugged.

He led me to the door and looked at the blood on my jeans. "Are you hurt?"

"No, it's her blood. The woman. Regulus..."

"Yes, something is wrong?"

"I recognize that woman. I've seen her picture before." I walked out the door without looking at him. "Listen, this is one of those things I'm too tired to think or talk about, but you know that I don't know my mother and she left us when I was a kid? Well, that was her. I think. I've seen pictures. I may have just met my mother."

I looked at his face and could tell he wasn't surprised.

Chapter Fifteen

Secrets to Portal

"Look," Regulus said, pointing up into the starry sky.

I leaned my head back to follow his gaze. "What? You gonna tell me the secrets of the universe?" My tone was forced at an attempt to sound light and mocking. I crossed my arms across my chest and tilted my head, waiting for his answer.

I didn't know why Regulus had stopped the car at the end of the road leading to my house. We were parked directly beside the waiting booth.

"No, I'm going to tell you the secrets to the portals," he answered matter-of-factly. He opened his door and stood. When I made no move, he leaned down and looked into the car. "Come on, I'm not going to kiss you again." Then he added softly, "Not tonight."

I could feel my cheeks heat at the thought. I

hurriedly jumped out of the passenger seat. "No, I didn't think that. At all."

He walked to my waiting booth, ducked to fit under the low roof and sat. He patted the seat beside him. "Then sit with me. I'll show you something."

All I could hear was my own breathing in the still night. I felt absurdly obvious. I tried to inhale and exhale calmly. I asked, "What were you pointing at up there?"

"The moon. See how it's a waxing crescent tonight?"

"Oh, yeah. My science project that I have been ignoring involved recording the moon phases and animals' eating patterns..." I faded off to stop myself from ranting on about my school project. He was smiling at me. I felt sillier.

"What about it?" I asked.

"The portals move every moon phase. Some move more than others."

I was shocked. "The one you came through. It's still here, right?" I looked over in the general direction of where the portal had been ever since my knowledge of it.

"Actually, no. That's what took Arizona so long. He had to travel to another portal location. One that had been mapped by the IIA."

I nodded. "We don't have one in Whispering Woods now?"

"I am positive that one still exists here. There has been a portal in your woods for as long as the IIA has been here. The IIA hasn't mapped it yet. We will, but it takes a little time."

"My woods. You mean our land?"

"This land near your home. Your portal has always been within a one mile radius of this location. Your waiting booth seems to be the epicenter of portal movement. You can find it."

I saw that he was looking at me expectantly. Waiting for some sort of reaction.

"No, I don't know why you think I can." I shook my head to emphasize my statement. I was embarrassed, and my throat was tight. I wiggled on the hard seat. I looked back up at the crescent-shaped moon, trying to absorb what he was telling me.

"Yes, you can, but you don't let yourself. You know that you feel the portal. You've denied your own nature. But your ability to feel and see what others can't...it makes you special. It's why the IIA has your genetic map on file. Your mother and brother are the same. It's recorded. Remember how you felt like you could hear a humming near the portal? Think back. Close your eyes." He brushed his fingertips lightly over my eyelids to close them. "What did you hear or feel or smell at the portal?"

He eased me back, and I felt the hardness of the waiting booth's wall on my side. I kept my eyes shut, trying to concentrate on remembering the things he asked me. The memories came easier with my eyes shut. I wouldn't have to look into his eyes.

"Um. OK. I don't know. I can't remember." My eyes were shut so tightly that I could feel the tiny wrinkles at the corners.

"You're trying too hard. You don't have to try. This isn't a pass or fail, a test of you. I think if you see that day in your mind, you'll remember certain sensations that you felt at the head of the portal."

I recalled the last time I went to the portal entrance with Regulus and Arizona. I was drawing a blank. I only remembered the thrill of riding on the motorcycle and hanging on to Regulus. I suddenly flashed back to an earlier time at the portal. It was the first time with Austin. I could see Biscuit in my mind's eye, twirling and barking excitedly. "I felt a vibration. I was drawn to it, like maybe...a moth is drawn to a warm light bulb." I opened my eyes and he was close, listening to every word. "That sounded stupid."

"No...no. Never stupid." I waited for him to continue. "What are you thinking about?" I asked.

"Kissing you again. Your eyes were closed, and it was very tempting. But I want you to trust me."

I opened my lips to interrupt him but he pressed his fingers over my mouth to stop my words that would spill out any minute.

"I want you to trust me like I trust you. You saved me from death."

Taking his hand away, I looked into his sincere blue eyes. "I think that's an exaggeration. I just put some ice packs on you."

"You protected me and sheltered me when I was vulnerable. You could have left me to be killed by the many who would do so. The IIA has many enemies."

"I'm scared, Regulus. I'm terrified of being part of this. I don't know why you have so much faith in me. I'm trying to trust you, but I need to know something. The truth. Do you and Arizona know where Pete is?"

He looked into my eyes, and I searched his face for any clue that I should doubt him.

"No, Mia, I don't. I'm relieved that I don't. I know that is not what you want to hear from me. You wish that I could give you the answers, but sometimes people don't want the truth."

I looked at him, glad that I could trust him, but I was heartbroken at the same time. He didn't know Pete's whereabouts.

My cell phone began to vibrate and play "Bad Boys." Austin. How had he done that? "Hey, where are you guys?" I asked him.

"Disposing of Bleeker's evidence," he answered. "I hope I wake up tomorrow and this was all a bad dream."

"I wish it could be, but I keep waking up and it's real," I said into the phone, and Regulus raised an eyebrow.

"We went by my house to get a shovel. I had to park a mile away so my parents wouldn't hear the engine. This stuff always looks easier in the movies."

"Where are you now?"

"Arizona knows of some place, actually on your land, called Potter's Field. Do you know what he's talking about?"

"No."

"Give the phone to Regulus. Arizona wants to talk to him. We need to let the professionals coordinate." He sounded snarky.

I handed my phone to Regulus and listened as he gave one word answers that left me clueless. When he finished the call, I was ready for some answers. "What's Potter's Field?"

"A place we've used for emergencies. I'll show you.

We can get fairly close in the car." He took my hand and led me back to the car. Again, he automatically went to the driver's side and at my look of exasperation, shrugged and grinned as if he couldn't help it.

Regulus reversed the car and returned to the highway leading toward Whispering Woods. Even though the sky was filled with stars, the night was dark without the artificial lights you find in civilization. The trees grew in solid walls along the sides of the road. Regulus turned the car onto a side road that was virtually invisible. The headlights cast an ethereal glow a few feet in front of us as we bumped along. The car dipped occasionally into potholes in the rarely traveled dirt road. An armadillo lumbered across the road, and Regulus slowed as it crossed.

A half mile later, Regulus pulled over and stopped.

"We have to wait now. Arizona will retrieve us."

As if on cue, the Jeep arrived. Regulus and I slid into the back seat. I sat behind Austin and his silence told me how his night was going. Arizona was back to his cheery self, all smiles. I wished Austin would say something...anything.

"I'm grossed out sitting on this seat and realizing that dead people were here earlier tonight. What happened to your cargo?" I couldn't help myself from asking.

"Deposited already. Actually, we've dug up a grave we're using," Arizona said it nonchalantly. The glow of the Jeep's dashboard cast some light in the darkness. I studied the back of Austin's head, trying to read his body language. Austin looked into the rearview mirror and made brief eye contact with me before concentrating on the road ahead.

"Not following what you're saying. If you've dug a hole in the ground to bury that poor woman and her baby, it won't work. Animals dig stuff up out here, Arizona. And it will be discovered by the police, and... Don't you watch CSI and television?"

"No," Regulus and Arizona said in unison.

Austin broke his silence. "We dug up an old grave, Mia. It's in a casket with another body." He said the words so low that I barely heard him.

"No, no, no." I started freaking out. "I don't know what you mean that you dug up somebody. You can't do that. Why is there a grave out here?" Nausea rolled over me and my face was going tingly. I curled into myself and scrubbed at my cheeks with my fists.

Regulus scooted over in the back seat until his leg touched mine. "You have to know about this place. There can't be any secrets in this. You may need to bring a body here sometime. Under different circumstances, it could be my body that you would dispose of." When I didn't answer, he put his hand on my knee and squeezed in reassurance.

Austin stopped the Jeep in the middle of the dirt road and turned to the back seat. "She's fine. Just let her get used to the idea for a minute." He stared at Regulus's hand on my knee.

We sat in silence. The Jeep idled and I sucked in deep gulps of air. All three sat looking at me while I sat and tried to breathe.

"OK, OK. Everybody quit staring. I need to move. This is making me crazy, sitting here like you're waiting for me to pass out," I said.

"Come then. Let's take her to this place," Regulus said more to Austin than to me.

We drove off road for a couple of miles before Austin stopped. Stepping out of the Jeep and into waist-high weeds, I followed as they walked ahead, walking along a path known only to Regulus and Arizona. Austin and I had ridden four-wheelers across most of my land, but I didn't recognize this area. Here, it was too overgrown to easily ride the ATVs. Tree branches hung low and I often had to duck. We walked for another half mile, and I fervently wished for a flashlight.

We came to a huge clearing. I could see headstones. "This has got to be the creepiest thing I have ever seen," I said.

"Yeah," Austin said. "I'd stay away from this place in broad daylight."

I looked up at him with only the moonlight and some stars, but all I could see were the whites of his eyes. I knew he felt as freaked as I did.

"If a Slip is dead and contaminated, or there is a risk of bringing something through the portal, we cannot take the body back. This is our Potter's Field," Regulus explained.

Arizona added, "We knew that you didn't know of its existence. It's apparent that these dead have been forgotten. The dead of your Earth. We borrow space. The IIA permits us to respect your traditions of burial. We buried the woman and child in a casket that has been here for a hundred years or more. I thought it was a nice touch."

I could see the dirt had been freshly dug up over one grave twenty feet from us. I looked at Arizona like he was crazy.

"There is no 'nice touch,' Arizona. This woman and her baby died. It has occurred to me that I could have stopped it from happening. I could have stopped whatever Dr. Bleeker did." My voice sounded so small and miserable.

"No, Mia." Austin sounded firm. "We didn't know that Dr. Bleeker would kill anyone. It's not your fault or my fault or anyone's fault."

"He's right. And it will be morning soon. You have to look to tomorrow and what has to be done in the future," Regulus said softly.

On those words, all four of us took one last look at the gravesite and turned to walk back to the vehicle. The sun would be rising soon.

***

I haven't pulled many all-nighters. It was something I was looking forward to as a college student. I imagined hanging out with my best buds while laughing and drinking Slurpees from the only twenty-four hour quick stop in town. In this vision, Em would stay in Whispering Woods and go to the "U." Austin would treat me like his little sister, like he had before, and I of course would maybe have a couple of new college friends. Cool friends who liked the same music, video games, and grape Slurpees.

I now sat in the passenger seat of my car looking across at Regulus, who had taken up permanent status as driver. Arizona sat in the middle of the back seat with his elbows propped on our seats talking about gene doping and Dr. Bleeker's possible whereabouts. Austin sat in his Jeep, glaring at Regulus.

I rolled down my window and turned to Austin. "Listen, I know you need to get home. Everything's going to look better in the morning. And I have to be home. If my dad makes it in before I do, I'll be grounded 'til

I'm thirty."

Austin nodded. His sleepy eyes told me that he was too tired to argue. He pulled out onto the dirt road, and I watched his taillights shrink into the distance. I leaned my head back against the seat and felt the car start moving. I closed my eyes.

"I have the updated portal coordinates," Arizona said quietly to Regulus. "We can get back to the Vault and report."

The car was silent, and I was almost asleep when I heard Regulus say, "We're leaving out the part about Mia's knowledge of Bleeker. He was a teacher she knew.

That's it. No more."

Arizona hesitated only for a moment. "Of course," he stated evenly.

***

"Hey my girl," my dad said as he ruffled my head.

I sat up with a start. A disorienting haze of memories swirled around in my head before I realized that I had been asleep on the couch. I couldn't remember getting into the house. I looked down to see that I was still dressed in the same clothes as yesterday.

"Hi Dad, missed you." I reached over to wrap my arms tightly around him. "How was your trip?"

"Too long. I have to stop taking these consulting contracts where they want me on-site so much."

"It's OK, Dad. I mean, I hope you weren't worried about me."

"No, I know you're not a kid anymore, sweetie." He ruffled my hair for a second time. "Pancakes?"

"Mmmm," I said, nodding my head with enthusiasm. "Please."

"Go wash your face and wake up then." He went to the kitchen.

I stared at my feet. I rose and went to look at the window.

I have the updated portal coordinates. The words echoed in my brain. I knew they were gone. I went upstairs to my room and brushed my hair back into the ponytail I usually wore. My computer screen was blinking with an IM from Austin, so I sat down to write Austin and Em a message to let them know that my dad was home and I'd talk to them both later.

To the right of my keyboard lay a small business card with a penny atop it. I had forgotten about the card from GameCon. I looked at the stack of cards that I had snagged from Dr. Bleeker's house. I set the card that was identical to the one I already possessed on top of the stack.

The card was plain, without a logo or anything to distinguish it from another. The name and address on the card meant nothing to me. No phone number or title for the person on the card. At the bottom, a web address didn't give me any more information than the rest of it. *www.aidosonearth.com.*

I typed in the address and waited. A company image and description loaded on the screen. "Genetically changing the world" was in bold font at the top. A picture of a young, attractive woman holding out a glass lab tube to her male counterpart took up most of the screen. A login section at the left caught my attention. Was it a website for employees or customers and not the public? There was not much to read or do if you couldn't log in.

I was about to give up for the moment and join my dad for breakfast when I saw something in the bottom section of the screen. A tiny animated logo inconspicuously teased my brain. It was a scientist, an Einstein likeness, holding a beaker while his head wove back on forth on his shoulders. He was a caricature with an enlarged bobbing head.

Memories flashed through my head...sitting in Dr. Bleeker's office with my science project logbook, thinking he was so quirky and nice, and looking at his collection of bobble heads.

It couldn't be a coincidence. I knew that Pete had left me the penny as a clue, but what did the card mean? Was it a warning? Or an invitation? I wondered what mysteries I might unravel in the future. At least I was confident that Pete was alive. The more complicating factor was the appearance of the woman I knew was my mother, a woman I didn't want to see.

A woman prepared to kill her own kid. Not that it mattered that she was my mother. I had no love for the woman who had wronged my dad and brother. They had loved her. I only needed to know how she fit into this puzzle. I wouldn't let her hurt them again.

"Mia, pancakes are ready," my dad yelled up the stairs.

I mentally filed away my discoveries for another time and bounded down the stairs. I ate my breakfast, absently forking up syrupy bites of pancake while nodding as my dad talked. After refusing a second helping, I showered and went outside with the excuse of gathering my memory cards for logging evidence for my science project.

I rode through the woods, wondering what Regulus and Arizona were doing. My head bounced as I drove too quickly on the golf cart over the bumps. I turned the steering wheel, circling around the previous location of the portal.

What if they didn't come back? That was the real issue. I had to see Regulus again.

I couldn't get his blue eyes, his voice, his kiss...out of my head.

With the golf cart almost out of fuel, I parked and made my way over to the waiting booth through ripples of dried golden weeds. The bench looked different in the daylight, not mystical or inspiring the telling of secrets as it had in the moonlight. I sat, leaning my head back and hearing Regulus's voice in my head. He had told me to remember the sensations that I felt at the portal. He had said that I could detect it. That I was born to do this.

I rose from the bench and walked slowly in the same circles that I had driven earlier. This time instead of filling my head with thoughts and worries, I tried to leave my mind a blank to be filled with sensations. I heard the songbirds and the wind. A light breeze tickled the hairs on my arms. The sun's warmth heated each skin cell on my face.

And then I felt the pull.

It was like a tiny cord that had been tied around my waist and yanked ever so slightly in one direction. I let myself walk toward the south, not in a hurry but as if I were letting the magnetic forces of the Earth take me wherever they pleased.

My ears pricked when I heard the hum. Barely audible at first, but the farther I walked, the louder it grew. It wasn't harsh or irritating. I had heard it before but dismissed it as background noise, noise that everyone hears.

But I now knew the difference. There was nothing here to make that noise. Nothing but the portal.

When I finally stopped walking, I looked down to see that I was standing near a flattened patch of grass identical to the earlier one, the only one I had seen. I felt coolness waft over the uncovered areas of my body like going into a cave from the heat of a one-hundred-degree day. The hum was comforting instead of disturbing as it had been the day that I had felt it with Austin and Biscuit.

I had found the portal entry. I was a human GPS after all.

I reclined at the edge of the circle of grass and threw my arm over my eyes, blocking out the noonday sun. My mind drifted into that state between dreams and reality. A feather-light touch caressed the side of my cheek. A light pressure on my lips. It happened so fast that I thought I might I have dreamed it.

I moved my arm and peeked through my lashes. "You came back."

"Of course I did."

He was so close I could see nothing more than indigo-colored eyes. I stared into them trying to read his intent. I knew I was a big ball of emotion, tumbling at high speed down a hill and I was afraid of crashing.

Looking into his eyes, I thought I knew him. His feelings. But that was all wrong, because I didn't know anything about him.

Then he leaned back, away from me a bit and I was sorry that the spell was broken.

"I wasn't sure. Were you sent back because you have more to do? More than find Dr. Bleeker and the Slips?" I was having trouble meeting his eyes and heard my voice sounding shaky. I'd rather not be a whiner, the type who begged for verbal reassurance. I took a deep breath.

"Your world is my post, and there is always more to be done." The words were businesslike, but his tone was not. It was silky and promising.

I sat up, attempting to clear my mind of the want for his kiss. He shifted to sit on the grass beside me. My eyes stayed on his bent knee instead of his eyes which seemed to bore into my soul.

"I really don't know where Pete is located. The IIA wants me to find him, though they are now satisfied with you stepping into his place." He paused and I met his eyes. I noticed a different tone in his voice. The confidence was gone. "This is a separate issue from what has happened between us."

"What has happened." I repeated the words, never

more unsure of myself than at this moment.

"This is a dangerous feeling for me to have." He took my chin and forced me to look into his face. He smiled crookedly, a rare treat for me. My stomach somersaulted.

When I didn't say anything, he continued, "It's against the rules, everything that I have been taught and believe. I could stop myself and stop these feelings that I have for you, but it would mean leaving this place."

"Do the IIA say you can't, well, umm...date?" I didn't know how else to phrase it since I wasn't sure about what to call it.

"They expect you to become our third. You're the gatekeeper for these portals in Whispering Woods."

"Gatekeeper? I thought you called it an enforcer. Enforcer sounds cooler." I hoped that teasing him would bring back his smile.

"Arizona and I are enforcers. The loyalty between enforcers and gatekeepers should be strong. We are a team. Allegiance is foremost to the IIA and to each other, but only as it strengthens the team. Relationships are not allowed between IIA operatives." He paused and offered his hand to me. With his thumb rubbing along the back of my hand, he added, "No one can know that my only desire at this moment is to press my lips on yours and hold your body against mine." He said the last part in a near whisper. His words would have been carried away on the wind if I hadn't leaned in, mesmerized by him.

"You guys have a law against dating? That's ridiculous."

"The IIA has good reason to prevent it. It will be our secret." He pulled me into his arms and murmured the last words against my hair.

"What about Arizona? He will know." I drew back to look at his face.

"Of course. We are safe with Arizona. I can trust him with anything. I'm constantly protecting him from his rule-breaking ways."

"What now?" I said, sighing in relief. "How about a date with a Whispering Woods U student?

Will your dad let you go out with an older guy?" "He's going to have to get used to me dating, first.

I usually hang out with Em and Austin." "I can do that. Hang." He grinned.

I was alarmed at the quickening of my heart. I was going to have to get used to that smile. I was in jeopardy of a stroke if I didn't. "Let's hang at my house then. Come on." I brushed the grass from my clothes and held out my hand to his. "Ever played *Quest of Zion?*"

"The game where you chase bad guys from another universe who plan to destroy your world?" He paused while I soaked in the irony of statement. "This should be easy. Do I have to take my eyes off of you to play?"

"Not required," I said with a grin, looking straight ahead and feeling hopeful.

The End

About the Author

Brinda Berry lives in the South with her family and two spunky cairn terriers. She's terribly fond of chocolate, coffee, and books that take her away from reality. She doesn't mind being called a geek or "crazy dog lady." When she's not working the day job or writing a novel, she's guilty of surfing the internet for no good reason.

Social media at:

http://www.brindaberry.com
https://www.facebook.com/BrindaBerryAuthor
https://twitter.com/#!/Brinda_Berry

For release news, subscribe at

http://www.brindaberry.com/mailing-list.html

www.ingramcontent.com/pod-product-compliance
Lightning Source LLC
Chambersburg PA
CBHW022045240626
47154CB00007B/2578